SPED

Re Marzullo

SPED

Cover design by JJ Wickham

Summary: Jack Parker has begun to wonder what happened to the "special" part of Special Education, or SPED, as he and his fellow SPED-ers must endure bullies, challenges from home and (most importantly to Jack) a lack of girls in their small group classroom. All of that changes in Jack's eighth grade year when girls and trouble show up. *SPED* shows middle school from the vantage point of a boy who has been content to sit on the sidelines but is realizing that growing up means taking chances not only for himself but for those he cares about.

Sauvignon Press

First Edition February 2013

ISBN 978-0-9889618-0-7

DEDICATION

To my amazing husband Tom E for his love and support and my children for their understanding when I couldn't come out to play.

ACKNOWLEDGMENTS

A big thanks to the over two thousand students I've had the pleasure of teaching and working with. Their youth and humor have kept me a perpetual adolescent. Thanks also to my all of cheerleaders/readers, but especially Kate and Stephanie, my language arts lifelines. Lastly a special thanks to my buddy Max with his ten-year-old's honesty.

CHAPTER ONE

So being dyslexic wasn't all bad, or at least it wasn't in first grade. Back then "dog" became "god" or "rat" became "tar" and I still got the general idea of things after some quick thinking and minor letter adjustments. No one but me knew that I wasn't learning to read just like everybody else.

Sadly though, by the end of fourth grade when "whimsical" became "smiwhilac," not even I, Jack Parker, Fake Learner Extraordinaire could pretend to learn anymore, and it was off to Special Education, SPED, I went.

First there was the mandatory "Your Kid Is In SPED" meeting with my parents. Looking back, I think my parents were actually glad that their average boy had something wrong with him. It gave them something to blame my lack of specialness on.

I mean, I wasn't ugly, but I wasn't handsome. I wasn't a clutz, but I wasn't a jock. I wasn't a social misfit, but I didn't have any real friends.

In other words, I wasn't here or there and had absolutely nothing that made me stand out in any way except my SPED label.

Since my dyslexia only affected my reading and not my writing, being in SPED for those last two years of elementary school just meant that an extra teacher came in my classes and helped me with my reading, and my school world really didn't change too much.

When I started sixth grade though, things changed overnight. I soon found out Hickory Hills Middle School, HHMS, had a small population of village idiots, and I was one.

In middle school there was no *extra* teacher in the room, there was literally an *extra* room with only other SPED-ers for classmates.

Coming into middle school and becoming a member of SGS (Small Group Superstars) actually wasn't too bad. While the other kids were flipping out trying to open their lockers and get through hallways jammed with frantic sixth graders, we (Small Group Studs – new name) stayed in a room with our teacher Ms. McFee and learned everything we needed to know.

The four of us did math and science and ultra boring social studies, but we did it at our pace and on our terms.

In the spring of sixth grade, we found out that we didn't have to take the Must-Pass state tests that the other kids did, and that suited me just fine. I'd seen too many freaked out kids on the bus during testing week. I remember one boy came to school with a dozen super sharp pencils, and he wouldn't let the teacher take any of them out of his sweaty hands.

Then he actually tried to poke her when she took them.

I decided right then that I didn't want anything to do with a test that made you want to assault adults.

So what if we didn't go to the sixth grade mixer or blender or whatever that dance was called? We had a calm, peaceful room where we'd slowly plod our way through the textbooks. Plus, if I have to be honest, I'll admit that staying out of the chaos of middle school has worked like a charm for me.

The bullies don't even know I'm here.

So I finished sixth grade, which was ultra chill and ultra easy – just the way I like school to be. Seventh grade was more of the same, though we did get one new customer in SPED-ville, Xinho.

Now I was sitting on the bus, riding to school for the first day of eighth grade after another boring summer and thinking about my SPED existence over the last two years. I listened to the excited kids around me talking about who might be in their classes or which teachers they hoped to get or hoped to avoid, and I didn't have a single question about this next year.

There was no wondering who would be in my class or who would be my teacher (it would be Ms. McFee again). I knew what to expect for eighth grade.

Exactly what to expect.

After two straight years of spending all day together, the SGS group had gotten to know what each other was thinking. We also knew, just by looking at one another, what each other was feeling. There was something kind of nice about people knowing you that well.

And something kind of suffocating.

As I got closer to school, I went through my (short) list of classmates in my head.

First there was Bryce who I've known since third grade. The other kids were scared of him, even Colin Markus the biggest jerk in the eighth grade stayed out of his way, though I'd never seen Bryce so much as raise a hand to anyone. I guess when you're six foot four in the eighth grade you didn't need to raise a hand to get respect.

Next was Skeever...or Weaver, as his parents like to call him. Skeever was a full-on, straight-up ADD-LD-HD-Red-Hot-Mess-D. He was a bag of bones – the poor kid never ate because of all the meds his parents kept him on – and could hardly make it to class in one piece, much less make it with any papers or pencils.

Next was my buddy Xinho who I mentioned earlier. Xin had the misfortune to be an Asian with learning disabilities. I'm not one to stereotype, but all the other Asians here at HHMS were absolutely brilliant and destined to be brain surgeons or computer engineers. My buddy Xin says all he wants to do is open a Chinese restaurant.

Last was Leo. What can I say about Leo? This poor kid wore T-shirts with dinosaurs on them (hello, it's eighth grade, man!), couldn't say his S sounds very well, and had blonde, curly hair. His cheeks were always red, and he always had a book clutched to his bony chest.

To say that the other kids were mean to Leo was like saying that the sky was blue. Of course it was and of course they were.

If I was invisible to the bullies, Leo wore a big red bull's-eye on his back.

Most kids looked away or tried to ignore the name-calling and silent shoves that happened when Leo was being bullied, and no one ever intervened. No one ever said, "shut up" to the Colins of the world.

No one.

Not even me.

I was nice to Leo in SGS and always helped him with his work or when he needed something, but I was ashamed to say I looked away in the outside world of our school.

Thinking about how I never stood up for Leo made me feel like something that should be scraped off the bottom of a shoe before it got tracked in the carpet.

Not good.

Anyway, that's our class. The Small Group Studs.

I'd never really paid attention to the fact that it's all boys in SGS, but heading to school for the start of eighth grade, that thought was front and center. Call it puberty or call it hormones or call it crazy, but I'd definitely noticed that instead of delightful-springtime-fresh-smelling girls being in my class, I had nasty-should-have-used-soap-smelling boys. Ugh.

This summer it (finally) hit me that we were an all boys club, and I wondered where all the dumb girls were.

Oops. I'm not supposed to call us dumb.

OK. This summer I wondered where all the Learning Disabled girls were because while girls might bring complications (at least according to the Disney Channel), they also bring a diversion. Something I could definitely use in my pretty boring life.

It had started when I'd seen cute girls at the pool this summer. They looked familiar from school, but since I didn't really know them, I'd been too shy to talk. That had gotten me thinking about trying to move out of SGS and back into a regular classroom (with girls), and I'd spent a lot of time trying to see the pros and cons of it all.

To leave our little room meant more stress AND it meant being out there with all the kids, the mean ones and the nice ones. Plus the workload was bound to be rough and I wasn't sure I could handle a faster pace.

BUT if I got out, I'd have more access to girls, which was something I thought about a lot lately.

My thoughts went back and forth like a ping-pong game in my head as I sat on the bus riding to school on the first day. Before I knew it, our bus driver had pulled into the parking lot and it was time to start another year – my *last* year – of middle school.

As I was getting off the bus, I saw Colin and his idiot friends in the bus lanes and headed towards Leo as he walked from his bus into the building. Leo was carrying the ever-present book and had a new backpack.

Part of me knew I should help Leo out somehow when Colin and those goons were harassing him, but the other part was like a chipmunk trying to stay away from a hawk. Just give me the closest hole – or in this case classroom – to duck into.

So I never got involved, never intervened, never stood up. I just tried to be as nice to Leo as I could when we were together in SPED-ville. I figured I'd made it through two years of middle school without a target on my back, so why stick my neck out now?

Awww...there was that bottom of the shoe feeling again...sigh.

As I walked with the rest of the herd of sleepy middle schoolers, I kept looking over at poor Leo. Colin the Colon stopped Leo as he tried to walk into the building.

"Hey SPED Head, is that a book on how to get smarter?" Colin asked Leo, pointing at the book.

"No," Leo responded, and he looked up with his round, blue eyes, "it's a book on dragon lore."

"Oooohhhh," Colin squealed. "Dragon lore." His lame friends all snickered and looked to him to see what was next.

The pack of wolves formed a semi-circle around Leo and refused to let him by. He searched all of their faces for help but saw nothing but scorn.

Luckily for Leo, Ms. McFee had a Bully Radar. Just as Colin was about to rip the book from Leo's hands, she came out of the building with her clipboard and whistle to send any bus riding slow pokes on to class.

"Everything all right out here?" she asked, eyeing Colin with suspicion.

Ms. McFee was no dummy, and she knew that poor Leo had a tough time at school. Unfortunately for him no teachers could ever catch Colin the Creep, and for some reason, Leo would never tell on him. This frustrated Ms. McFee to no end, and I'd heard her telling Leo before that he "could tell her anything." But he just looked at her with those big, blue eyes and said that everything was fine.

The fact that Leo had been picked on before the first day of school even started – and by a pack of douchebags no less – was a very bad sign of things to come. I walked into Ms. McFee's room wishing that a bus filled with all of the bullying victims from HHMS would run Colin down.

And soon.

Walking into SPED-land was like going into your grandma's house when it smelled like cabbage. It wasn't the best place to be, but it wasn't the worst either.

The room hadn't changed much over the summer – oh wait, McFee got a new poster of some kittens hanging on a tree limb. "Hang in there, baby."

Ha. Good advice for Leo.

For the past two years, our SGS had been a well-oiled machine. We knew where to sit. We knew who answered which questions (I did math, Skeever handled English, Xin rocked science, Leo loved social studies, and Bryce...well never mind Bryce). We knew everyone's habits and quirks. We knew Bryce's mom cooked beans every Sunday night (whew) and we even knew when McFee had a date coming up.

On Date Days she was flustered and always checking her computer. On Days After Date Days she was either cranky or super happy. Go figure.

Yeah, after two years of together time, I'd say the SGS knew each other's rhythms and habits. For better or worse, we were as close to married as five guys could get. Or maybe we're like brothers. Being an only child, I wasn't sure what that whole sibling thing was about, but I pictured it something like this only without the sharing-the-bathroom part.

So imagine my face as I walked into the first day of eighth grade in our same ole room on the same ole hall and I didn't find the same ole peeps. Instead, I found not one but *two* new faces in our midst.

Two (gulp) girl faces.

The first face was small and light brown. She looked about eight years old and seriously pissed.

The second face was the stuff dreams were made of...

CHAPTER TWO

I think when I first saw The Angel my mouth dropped open and maybe some spit sloshed out.

By the time I realized I should close my pie hole, everyone was looking at me weirdly. Even Bryce had noticed and was staring at me for a long second before he looked to Harper.

I'd never seen a girl so beautiful. The girls from the pool were pretty, but this girl was in another league. She was NFL compared to peewee football. Olympics compared to "race you to the corner." Iron Chef compared to my mom's tuna surprise.

The pool girls weren't even in the same galaxy.

First off, she was almost radiant looking and not covered in a ton of makeup. Some of the girls at HHMS pile on so much black stuff around their eyes they look like zombies, or wear so much powder they look pale like a fish belly or orange like an Oompa-Loompa. This girl was so pretty that I think my eyes started watering.

Though that could've been my allergies.

Whatever it was, all I wanted to do was stare.

And I was.

Just staring.

So I dropped my backpack down on my desk and coughed and pretended I was choking so I could go get some water. I needed to get a grip for sure.

Walking out into the hall, I heard Leo say, "I hope he's all right..."

And a squeaky female voice answered, "Aw, he's fine, he just got scared by Goldilocks here."

And Squeaky Voice was right. I'd never been so close to a girl so breathtakingly (Ohmygod what's wrong with me...how goofy am I sounding??) beautiful.

Before I had run away to get water, our eyes had met briefly and she looked up at me with her sparkling green eyes. (Ohmygod I said sparkling.)

After I got the water I stood by the door to calm down (A Pretty Girl In SPED!) and I could hear McFee explaining that SGS stood for Small Group Superstars and that basically meant being in this room all day and learning with these same people.

"So I never leave here?" I heard The Angel say. "What about lunch?"

"Well we decided last year that rather than wait in the long lines at lunch in the cafeteria, we'd grab our lunch early and then eat in here or sometimes go outside."

No one said that the main reason we chose to eat in our room was to keep Colin and his pack of rabid dogs from preying on Leo. Plus it was easier to avoid being singled out as the SPED-ers if we get our lunch first before any of the regular ed customers.

I walked back in the room doing a fake cough to cover my freak-out of the moment before, but I didn't dare look at The Angel in case I started choking all over again. I didn't want to sound like a cat with a fur ball, so I kept my eyes down.

McFee continued, "Of course we leave here other times, too. We go out to the restroom or to the library or computer labs. But the majority of our time's spent in here."

At that, the small girl interjected, "But it smells like a monkey's butt in here!"

"Bernadette!" Ms. McFee said as she tried not to laugh. "We really don't say things like 'monkey's butt,' OK?"

"OK...it smells like a monkey's armpit then. Open the damn window, would ya?"

"Bernadette!" Ms. McFee was frowning now. "We don't say damn either!"

"So you just smell like monkey butt...sorry...like stuff... and no one cares? Crazy." Bernadette turned her head towards The Angel and took a sniff. "You the only one in here smells like folks should."

At that we all looked at one another self-consciously and I saw Xinho give his armpit a sly sniff.

Ms. McFee apologized for our smell to our newest members, "I'm sorry Bernadette, but the windows don't open. I can see if we have some air freshener or something."

The red face on all of us slowly faded, and we were all adjusting to our new classmates (girls in SPED!) when the speaker in the ceiling made its morning squawk.

"Beeeeeeepppppp. Good Morning, Hickory Hills Middle School," came the voice of our principal, Mr. Feathers.

Out of habit, we all stood when we heard the announcements begin and joined in the Pledge of Allegiance. Even The Angel mouthed the words silently.

After the pledge, Principal Feathers began to blab on about how excited he was for the first day of the "best year ever." I'm pretty sure last year was supposed to be the best year, but who's keeping track? I really didn't have much of an opinion on the principal since he wasn't part of my day-to-day HHMS routine. I just knew that he yelled at kids for leaving trash on the ground or not following the dress code.

Just then I heard him say something about "chicken pot pie" for lunch, so I knew that the announcements must be almost over.

Almost over, but unfortunately not quite. Principal Lame-O always finished his announcements with his "words of wisdom." More like "Words to Immediately Forget" or "Words of Stupidity," but he said this junk every day.

"As we begin another great school year, our character word of the month is Respect. I know that it's important to have respect for one another and yourselves," came the voice from the speaker.

What a crock. Principal Feathers had kids torturing other kids just because they looked different or dressed different, and all he did was yammer on about respect.

Why didn't he do something about the Colins of the world?

Why didn't I do something?

No comment.

At that moment, Feathers ended the announcements with "make it a great day or not, the choice is yours." Another crock. I'd heard that statement every day I'd been at HHMS, and I'd definitely decided to have great days a lot more often than they had really happened. Sometimes it just isn't in your power to have a great day no matter how hard you try.

After the Commander of Crap finished, we all sat down and looked expectantly at Ms. McFee.

"Welcome back, everyone," she said, looking at us. "And a special welcome to our new students, Harper and Bernadette."

"Bernie," barked the small, wiry girl sitting in what used to be my seat. "I go by Bernie."

"No problem, Bernie." Ms. McFee made a little note in her attendance folder and then looked up.

"I'd like to welcome you two to our group and welcome back our regular students from last year," she said, smiling.

"And I'd also like to start today with some introductions," she continued. "Let's each say our names, and then two unusual things about ourselves...then the next person will recite the others' names and facts and add theirs to the list...then we can all learn each others' names and learn fun facts about one another!"

"But Ms. McFee, we know every..." Leo piped in immediately.

I nudged him under the desk with my foot and he hushed. I wanted to learn anything I could about Harper (I'd already memorized her name and pictured it in a tattoo on my bicep), and if McFee wanted to waste time with lame name games, that was fine with me.

"OK...I'll start," began McFee. "I'm Ms. McFee and I eat sunflower seeds every day, and I like to listen to '80s music."

Not exactly unusual for an old person to listen to old music, but OK. Rock on, McFee.

Leo figured out that I wanted to play this game – he's quick like that - so he jumped in next. "That's Ms. McFee, she eats seeds and listens to old music. And I'm Leo, and I sleep under my bed and am writing a book."

Everyone looked at him on that one. Under the bed??? I should probably ask him about that later.

Next came Skeever. "So, OK, that's McFee, I mean Ms. McFee and she eats seeds and listens to bad music. Next is Leo who sleeps on the floor and is a writer. I'm Skeever and I'm on new meds and don't sleep at all."

We all laughed, and I looked around nervously for whoever would step up next.

Xinho rescued us. "That's Ms. McFee and she eats sunflower seeds every day while she listens to bad 80's big hair bands. That's Leo who sleeps under his bed for some reason while working on his book. That's Skeever who's taking new meds that don't let him sleep at all. And I'm Xinho. The only dumb Asian you'll ever meet. But I'm a good cook."

Ms. McFee started to say "Xinho...you aren't..." But he beat her to it.

"Ok. So maybe I'm not dumb, but I'm definitely not smart enough for an Asian."

"Xinho!"

"Sorry McFee, just calling it like I see it. How about I'm Xinho and I love to cook and I'm not Chinese or Japanese, I'm actually from South Korea."

"Really? See guys, we're getting to know more about each other! I think it's great that we know more about your heritage, Xin. Next?" McFee looked around expectantly.

There was only Bryce who never talked, me, and the two new girls left, so I stepped up, clearing my throat.

"Um, hi, so that's Ms. McFee. She eats sunflower seeds every day as you can tell by the shells around her desk. She also listens to '80s music as you can tell by her screensaver of Big Haired Guys."

I wanted to let The Angel know that I paid attention, so I was adding details.

"Next is Leo who sleeps under his bed as you can tell by the dust bunnies on the back of his shirt," as I said this one, Xin brushed Leo's back off quickly. "You can also tell that Leo is writing a book because he's always got that spiral notebook with him."

The group looked impressed with my powers of observation. All except Bernie, who wasn't looking at me, but was looking out the window instead.

"That's Skeever," I continued. "He's on new meds as you can tell by his feet tapping out a nonstop beat, and he doesn't sleep as you can tell by the bags under his eyes."

"After Skeever is Xinho who likes to cook as you can see by his brownbag lunch. He never buys food in the cafeteria."

"That's not food they're serving. It's garbage that wouldn't fit in the dumpster," said Xinho.

"And Xin is also from South Korea, which you can tell by the flag patch on his backpack."

I was on a roll with my extra details. I felt like a detective on *Law and Order* getting ready to tell who the murderer was.

"And I'm Jack. There isn't much that's unusual about me except that I have dyslexia and I want to be a forensic scientist when I grow up."

I thought it was a good idea to get my Learning Problem out there so that The Angel knew I wasn't Severely Messed Up. Just Moderately Messed Up. Plus I was letting her know that I had plans for my future and wasn't just some slacker.

"Thank you, Jack. Good job with all the extras," Ms. McFee said. "Who wants to go next?"

Bryce stood up and said, "I'm Bryce," and then he sat down. Done.

"Thanks Bryce!" McFee was psyched that he'd said two words together. Or really three if you split up "I'm."

We all looked at Harper and Bernie since they were the only ones left.

"I'll go next," came the squeaky voiced one. "So, that's the teacher and she eats squirrel food and listens to bad music. Her name is Miss McBee."

"McFee."

"Sure thing. McBee," Bernie said, pushing McFee's buttons on day one. This could be an interesting year.

"So after McBee we got Leo who has issues with his bed, Skeever who has issues with his meds, and Xinho who has issues."

Everyone laughed and McFee didn't correct her.

"After that is Bryce, who's the strong, silent type, and then my man Jack who has dyslexiwhozits," she paused and looked me up and down. "Which I'm pretty sure means he's got the hots for Goldilocks here."

CHAPTER THREE

Everyone laughed and I felt the blood rushing to my face. Harper put her head down and smiled. Or maybe she was trying not to throw up.

Bernie looked me straight in the eye and had a smirk on her face. "Just tryin' to keep it real in here, people," she said. "OK. I'm Bernie. I've lived in forty-four houses in thirteen years and you don't want to mess with me." She sat down and we all believed her warning despite her being four foot something and so small I could fit her in my pocket.

After Bernie and her bombshell, we all stared at Harper and waited for her to stand and introduce herself.

She sighed and pushed her long, blonde hair back off of her face. "OK," she began. "That's Ms. McFee and she has lovely skin though pink's not her color. Next is Leo who has the longest eyelashes ever. Super jealous."

Leo got a compliment! How did that happen!? I thought Leo was going to pass out with happiness, and he tried to blink quickly and see his own eyelashes.

"After Leo came Skeever who's wearing a T-shirt of one of my favorite TV shows."

All heads swiveled to Skeevs and we saw that his T-shirt was advertising "Spongebob Squarepants." She likes kids' cartoons?

"Then we had Xinho who wants to be a chef and today has teriyaki chicken with ginger for his lunch and it smells delicious."

"And then there's Bryce who doesn't talk much but is rocking some hot kicks." Again all heads turned to see Bryce's shoes, which were just a pair of Converse and not that hot in my opinion.

"Of course that's Bernie who I totally don't want to mess with but would love to have on my side in case of emergency," Bernie gave a little nod of approval.

"Finally there's Jack who's a little full of himself," she said, laughing at me. "See, I pay attention to details, too."

Wait, that wasn't a compliment! Everyone else got a compliment – nice eyelashes and hot kicks and good in a fight – but I got "full of himself?" What gives?

"So, hi everybody. I'm Harper and I didn't want to move away from my old town, I guess that's not so unusual, and I love to watch professional hockey."

"That was wonderful, everyone! I just know we're off to an awesome year together." McFee clapped as she said this and went around the room looking for high fives.

She was so delighted that we'd all played her First Day of School Get to Know You Game that she let us take a water break even though we'd only been in school for half an hour.

As we walked out the door and down the hall, I was about to get up the nerve to ask Harper where she moved here from, but Bernie beat me to it.

"So you move a lot, too, huh?" Bernie asked her.

"No, not usually. My dad just got sent overseas for his job, and I couldn't go with him. That means I have to live with my mom for now. I'm not even sure how long I'll be here."

"I get it," Bernie said.

"What about you? Why do you move so much?" Harper asked as she leaned over the fountain to get a drink.

"Well, I can't seem to find a foster home that I like and that likes me back. There's always something wrong with one end of the deal, so I keep moving. This family I'm with now seems OK though."

"Wow. I thought I had it rough moving here. That really sucks, Bernie. Sorry," Harper said.

"It is what it is," Bernie said and laughed at her own comment. "Some foster dude used to say that when his wife burned the dinner. I kind of like it. It really doesn't mean much, but it fits my life perfectly. It is what it is."

Harper nodded in agreement and turned around to look at me.

"So you're Jack and you're dyslexic. What does that mean exactly?"

Aghhh. The Angel was talking to me. Directly. I guess I better get used to that since she was bound to talk to me a lot with only seven of us in a room.

"Um, well, it means that letters get mixed up when I'm reading. I don't always see the same words other people do, so it takes me a bit longer to get through stuff. I can write okay, but reading is rough."

"Got it. I have most of my problems in math. It's like The Black Curtain of Doom comes down in my head when I have to do number stuff. It just shuts my brain down."

"Wow. I can do numbers just fine. No dyslexia at all there. Maybe I can help you with your math, and you can help me with my reading."

Bernie was trailing along behind us as we went back to SPED-ville, and she piped up, "I know exactly what's wrong with me. I'm never at a school long enough to learn my locker combination...you can forget learning what the other kids are doing. Never happen."

We all agreed, and Bernie definitely had a point. How could you ever keep up if you kept moving all the time? No wonder she was in with us.

"So you really stay in one room all day? Every day?" Harper asked as we were walking back into our classroom.

"Yeah. We do," I answered.

"No offense, but that sounds horrible," Harper replied. "At my old school I was in regular classes, but they had an extra teacher to help the math dummies."

"Yeah, I did that in elementary school, but here they are super big on keeping their test scores up, so they keep us apart from the other students. That way we don't have to take the big state test and damage Principal Feathers' perfect record of 100% passing."

"So we're stuck in here because of testing? That's ridiculous!"

"Well, to be honest, we really don't mind so much. HHMS can be a rough place."

Bernie looked at the sparkling clean halls with cheerful posters on the walls and gleaming floors. "Rough my ass. Looks like an ad for Mr. Clean to me."

"I mean the students. There's some really mean kids here – I mean beyond total jerks – who like to pick on Leo especially. Being separate keeps him safer. Hopefully high school will be better," I said and we walked silently for a minute.

"Hold on, you have to wait til high school to get out..." Harper began.

Just then Ms. McFee poked her head out of the classroom door and told us to get a move on. We walked in the door just as another teacher let her kids out for a water break, and I could see Colin looking at Harper with obvious interest.

Behind Colin I saw Britney Starks staring at Harper with curiosity and, I'm sure, some jealousy since Harper was so pretty. I noticed that all the kids were noticing us more than usual ("Hey look, it's the SPED freaks!") as we walked back into our room, and I knew what the buzz was about.

New Kids.

HHMS was one of those schools in one of those towns that people didn't come and go from. Living here was kind of a life sentence, at least until you got old enough to go to college and get the heck out. Most of us had been together since kindergarten or first grade, so we knew who was who and what was expected of us.

To get new students at our school was like throwing raw meat to a pack of lions. It stirred things up and brought out the competitive side of kids.

Unfortunately for our two new kids, they were stuck in SPED-land with us.

Definitely not cool.

Double unfortunately for Harper was the fact that she was pretty and Britney didn't like competition. Two years ago, we got a cute new girl named Anna who was a better cheerleader (and much nicer person) than Britney would ever be. Poor Anna didn't even make it to Christmas before her parents pulled her out and sent her to private school.

Britney and her group of morons made Anna's life so miserable that she couldn't take it. They wrote stupid

25

lies about her on the walls in the bathroom, whispered when she walked by then burst out laughing, and put glue in her locker combination so it wouldn't open up.

You know, Welcome To The Neighborhood type activities for sure.

Of course they never proved who was doing those mean things, but everyone knew. No one messed with Britney. She was the salt to Colin's pepper. God help the world if they grew up and had babies. Those would be the meanest kids alive.

When we went back to class, Ms. McFee had a journal writing prompt on the board, and we spent the next half hour writing about "What we expect to accomplish in our last year of middle school." McFee was big on us writing journals, but I didn't mind so much.

I wondered if she really read them all. I once stuck some random insults (butthead, boogerbrain, sewerbreath) in my journal entry, and she didn't even circle them with her purple pen. Either she didn't read them, or she blamed them on my dyslexia. Hard to say.

The first day of school progressed pretty normally. We went to lunch early so we could beat the rush and the stares, then we had a rousing game of "polynomial bingo" in the afternoon to brush out the "summer math cobwebs" as McFee called them. I sat by Harper and helped her with some of the problems. I think her arm brushed mine once...either that or I got shocked by static electricity.

For sure I knew that I could smell her perfume. I planned on going home and tearing through my mom's magazines with all their perfume ads till I discovered the smell that was Harper.

Would it be weird if I sprayed that smell on my pillow at night (yes)?

Would it make me dream of Harper (no)?

Wow. I was a goner after only seven hours of being in the same room as her.

By 3:20 we were all French fried after our first day of school. Summer made you lazy, so having to use our brains all day was new and not so pleasant. Though having two new faces in the room to liven things up was really great.

I realized then that what I'd been wishing for on the bus – seeing more girls than just the ones at the pool – had come true. There were finally girls in SGS! I guess that meant I had to actually start combing my hair instead of just putting my fingers through it, but it was totally worth it.

Finally Principal Feathers came on for the afternoon announcements. Why he had to use precious afternoon time to repeat the same stupid announcements he made in the morning was something I didn't get.

At the end of the school day, no one was listening to him drone on about the Naturalist Meeting that would be held next Tuesday in the gym. No one paid attention, not even Ms. McFee. It looked as if she was checking her email.

A Date Night? Maybe.

The magic words of dismissal came and we trooped out the door. I headed to my bus, but I noticed Harper walked to the front of the school with Xinho. She must be a car rider because I couldn't imagine her using those dainty feet to walk. I guess her mom would be picking her up every day. I knew from this morning that she wasn't on my bus with me, but I'd kind of hoped that we could walk to the buses together.

Just in front of me, Leo walked with Bernie and showed her his newest book when Colin and his group of living dead came out from between two of the parked buses.

"Hey dumbass," Colin began as he blocked Leo's path. "We didn't get to finish our conversation this morning. I'm pretty sure you were going to tell me about dragons or some gay stuff like that."

Bernie took in the scene. She knew immediately that Colin was a jerk, and she said loudly "Hey man, what's happenin?" and put her hand up for a high five.

A puzzled Colin instinctively smacked his hand to hers, but in an instant she grabbed him by the hand and began squeezing his backwards at the wrist so hard it made him gasp. She did it so quickly and so subtly that I doubt anyone even knew what was going on. They looked like two friends cutting up except for the look of panic on Colin's face.

"Great to meet you. I'm new here, and any friend of Leo's is a friend of mine."

That's all she said. When she dropped his hand, Colin stared at her openmouthed and rubbed his injured wrist with the other hand. His crew was confused about what had happened, and Colin sure didn't want to tell them that a puny little black girl had just about broken his wrist.

Instead he grunted, "Later," and motioned for the group to move on.

I caught up to them and looked at Bernie in shock.

"You probably shouldn't have done that. Colin's the biggest jerk and bully this school has."

"Maybe he shouldn't have talked to my friend like that," Bernie answered with her eyes flashing and her hands on her hips.

"Friend?" Leo said with a look of delight on his face.

"Yeah, it looks like you might need one in this crazy ass place."

As we continued trooping to our separate buses, I saw Colin and his friends pointing at Bernie.

The best part? She pointed right back.

CHAPTER FOUR

All the way home on the bus I thought about what Bernie had done. She'd been at our school for seven hours and had already taken on the biggest bully in the place. Was she crazy or was she a hero? Was I right for laying low around Colin or was it back to the bottom-of-the-shoe feeling?

I think I knew the answer to that one.

I got home right on schedule (our bus driver is big on keeping on schedule even if it means running a few lights), dropped my backpack on the kitchen floor and went straight to the refrigerator.

Unfortunately my mom was a health food fiend, so her idea of a great after school snack was lentil chips and hummus. I was tempted to just ignore my growling stomach, but lunch (such as it was) had been hours ago.

Even though I hated the cafeteria food, I bought lunches anyway. In elementary school I was asked too many times to identify weird things in my lunchbox ("It's freeze-dried seaweed.") so now I eat tater tots and mystery meat every day.

Can't wait til I can drive. I'll go by McDonald's twice a day.

I chilled out in front of the TV and heard my mom opening the garage door about half an hour later. She and my dad have their own business. It's a paint supply store that also features antique-style wallpaper – exciting, right?

My parents work together, but they always ride to work in separate cars. They say it's because he likes talk radio and she prefers top-forty music, but my dad once told me that he hated to ride in the car when my mom was driving, and since she got carsick, she always had to drive.

"Hey honey," she yelled from the kitchen. "How was the first day?"

"It was good," I answered. No way was I telling her that there was a pretty new girl in my class. She'd ask me about her every day and wonder when I was going to invite her over to play Scrabble or something lame.

"You know," I continued. "Same room and same teacher and all. Though we did get a new girl, Bernie, and she should be pretty entertaining."

"Well, school is mostly about learning and not about being entertained. I hope she won't be a distraction," mom said as she stood in the doorway looking at me. My mom was the best joy-sucker I knew. She was always looking at the bad instead of trying to see the good.

Though I had to admit that she was right about the distraction part. If she only knew what was really distracting me! I'd spent most of the afternoon trying to stare at Harper with my head down and gave myself a headache from using only my peripheral vision.

Forget doing the lessons. All I wanted to do was gaze (Ohmygod I said gaze) at her. Hopefully tomorrow would be easier.

"So I guess this year's all about getting ready to go into big classes in high school," I said as she came into the living room and picked up the mail off the front table.

"What do you mean big classes?"

"You know. Regular classes where I'll be with the other kids and not just a few SPED-ers," I told her.

"Honey, don't say SPED-ers. It sounds like a bug."

"OK. Fine. I'll be with other kids and not just my small group. I figure in high school, I'll go back with other kids like in elementary school."

When I said that, she stopped sorting bills, looked at me from across the room, and said, "Jack, based on what the principal said at our last meeting to discuss your progress, you won't ever be in big classes. They just go too fast in the regular classes and they're afraid you'd get behind."

I stopped eating and stared at her. "Wait. Are you saying they want to keep me locked up in small group all the way through high school?"

"That's the way I understood it, honey," she said as she began rustling around the kitchen to start dinner. "The school knows what's best for you, Jack. I have to trust them."

So I'd *never* get out of SGS? That couldn't be right. I'd ask my dad when he came home. Surely he'd see that four more years of Small Group Sameness wouldn't be in my best interest.

"Um, hey mom. Where are all of your old magazines? I need some pictures for a collage for school," I fibbed from the couch. I still hoped to figure out what perfume Harper was wearing and get some of my own.

Wow. Now even *I* think I'm weird.

My dad came home about an hour later while I was at the table pretending to look for collage pictures, but really I was trying to identify Harper's unique scent.

I swear I'm not as creepy as that just sounded.

"Hey, Dad," I called as he came in.

"JackAttack. How goes it buddy?" My dad had a nickname for everyone and about twenty for me.

"Pretty good. School sucks, but hey, you know, it's a living." That was another one of our jokes. Anything unpleasant can be "a living." Taking out the trash, doing dishes, cleaning the garage. All can be categorized as a living. I know it doesn't make sense, but most of what my dad says never makes sense.

"Ha!" he laughed. "You got it, buddy. Enjoy school while you can. The workaday world can be very treacherous. Very treacherous indeed."

That was hilarious since my dad sold paint, and the most treacherous thing he might encounter was a stray brush or a paint roller out of whack, but I let him have his laugh.

"So dad," I jumped right in, "Mom says I don't get to leave SGS when I'm in high school next year. That can't be right."

Now it was his turn to shuffle through the mail, and I didn't think he even heard me.

"OK," he said, flipping through his latest Science Digest magazine.

"No, Dad. It's not OK."

"What?" he responded, finally focusing on me again.

"The fact that I won't be allowed out of SGS and into bigger classes when I get into high school."

"I'm afraid I don't know much about that, Jack. Your mom went to your last annual meeting with the principal, but I didn't go because we couldn't leave the store. I'm sure they talked about it, and we usually just do what the school recommends. It's their business, you know."

"No. I'm pretty sure it's *my* business," I replied, starting to get angry.

"Hey, now. Simmer down, Jack. What's the deal about getting out of SGS? I thought you preferred life in the slow lane."

"Maybe I used to prefer it. But four years in high school stuck with the same kids? That sounds like torture to me."

"I hear you, buddy. Let me talk to your mom about it and we can see what's what." He clapped me on the shoulder as he walked past me to go upstairs. "You're right to be thinking ahead...there won't be any cute girls in SGS in high school, and that could definitely be a bummer."

Ha! If only he knew.

At dinner that night, I decided to let on that we had two new students, but I figured I'd just forget to tell them that Harper was a girl. Harper kind of sounded like a boy's name, and that way I could talk about her/him but not get pestered by my mom's nosy questions.

"So Bernie, the new girl, keeps calling Ms. McFee Ms. McBee. It's pretty funny," I said in an effort to keep them from talking about something ridiculous like the economy or the new paint colors the store just got.

"It sounds disrespectful to me," my mom said.

"Aw hon, lighten up. It's just kids testing boundaries. I remember I used to call one of my teachers Mr. Pickles instead of Mr. Rickles, but his hearing was so bad he was never sure what I was saying," Dad added.

"Wow, dad. What a rebel!" I laughed across the table.

"Your father used to be a bad boy before he met me," Mom said. "Cutting class to go for cappuccinos and riding his moped without a helmet,"

"Whoa...surprised you didn't go straight to juvie, Dad, with shenanigans like that."

My dad just smiled and didn't say a word. Something told me he'd gotten up to some serious shenanigans, but he couldn't tell me about them. Not yet anyway.

"So Mom, you will talk to Mr. Feathers about me getting out of SGS for next year, right?"

"Jack what's causing all of this? Why all of a sudden do you want to get out? You've done so well the last the last two years in SGS."

My dad looked at Mom and said, "It comes down to one thing, Sofie"—he paused for effect—"Girls."

I almost spit out my milk I was so startled to hear him catch on so fast, but I faked like I didn't know what he was talking about. "Dad, I don't want to see more girls." Just this one girl, I thought to myself.

"Just because I'm special ed doesn't mean I have to be locked away in a closet," I continued. "And besides, I know I'll have a better chance at getting into a good college if I take regular classes in high school."

My parents made eye contact, and neither one spoke for a second.

"Jack, you know college isn't for everyone," my mom began.

"Yeah, JackSmack, there are lots of jobs that don't require college," Dad agreed.

"Sure, a garbage man or a used car salesman. Hardly what I'd call fulfilling careers."

"Now honey," my mom began and my parents looked at one another again.

"Mom, you know I talk all the time about wanting to be a forensic scientist. I think I'll need more than a high school diploma for that," I said angrily.

"OK. I thought that was just a phase, like when you wanted to be a bulldozer driver," Mom said.

"Very funny. I definitely plan on going to college to study forensic science." I said and looked at both of them. "Seriously, since when am I not going away to school?" I asked, and no one said anything for a minute.

"Well, since the principal told us last year how it usually works out for kids like you in the SPED track," my mom finally said, looking sad and uncomfortable.

"Like Feathers the Feeble would know anything about kids like me," I kept right on before my mom tried to say that calling the principal "feeble" was distracting or disrespectful. "He never comes in our classroom or talks to Ms. McFee about us. It's like we aren't even there...tucked away in our stupid little room," I said, getting angrier every second.

"Jack, I can't believe you're getting so upset about this," my mom said, cutting into her chicken. "You still get to go to high school and get a diploma and then come to work at the shop with your dad and me."

Work at their store?! Was she crazy?! I couldn't take a day around those fumes and fussy women trying to decide between Lemon Yellow and Yellow Lemon.

"Can I be excused please? I'm not hungry anymore. Going to go study for my garbage man aptitude test."

"Jack," my mom began as I stomped upstairs to my room.

"No. Let him go, Sofie," Dad said.

I slammed the door and flopped down on my bed. Spend my life in a paint store? Not hardly.

Maybe Harper was right. Maybe it was time to get out of SGS for good.

CHAPTER FIVE

Of course I went back to school and completely forgot my vow to get out of SGS. Once I was back in the comfortable room with Harper and Bernie and the guys I'd known forever, the thought of getting into regular classes just didn't enter my head again until a couple of weeks later when we had a mandatory all-school assembly to hear a program on anti-bullying.

Normally Ms. McFee could get us out of attending most assemblies. She'd tell them it wouldn't work with our schedule or that it would disrupt our day, but this time Principal Feathers wouldn't budge. He was having the local news come in and report about the HHMS "No-Bully Zone" that he'd decided to create, and all students had to attend this stupid assembly.

I guess even dummies looked good on camera.

The real deal was that if he thought hanging up some posters and leading a pep rally would cure what was wrong with this school, he's nuts. Til the Britneys and Colins move on to high school, there would always be bullying here.

Of course, when they move on, some other jerk-offs will come in and take their place.

And so it goes, the Circle of Middle School Life.

The assembly was supposed to start at 9:30, and at 9:42 Ms. McFee let out a shriek.

"Oh, no. How did it get so late?" she said as she looked at the time on her computer.

"Come on, guys. We were supposed to head to the theater fifteen minutes ago! Crap!"

McFee doesn't say things like crap, so this wasn't good, and we all hustled out the door.

Bernie was the last to come and was complaining the whole way. "Why do we got to waste our time in a no-bully assembly? I can tell you how to get to a no-bully zone...kick that bully's ass. That will put them in a zone all right."

"Bernie, please stop saying ass," McFee said over her shoulder.

We finally made it to the theater and heard a voice booming on the other side of the doors.

"Maybe we can just slip in," Leo said. "No one will notice that we're late."

If only. When McFee opened the doors, it was dead quiet in the room and Principal Feathers had just said, "Who here's been a victim of bullying?"

And in came the SPED-Parade. Right on cue.

The theater burst into laughter at our expense, and my face got hot with shame to be seen with this group of "dummies." I ducked my head so no one could see me in the dark theater.

It was at that moment I remembered my vow to get into regular classes and out of SGS.

McFee motioned for us to sit in an empty row near the center of the theater, and we felt every eye in the place on us. There were still some whispers going on when we finished our Walk of Shame, and I was thankful to finally sit and attempt an anonymous hunching of my shoulders. I think if I'd worn my hoodie, I totally would've pulled it over my head.

For a kid who'd tried to stay invisible for two years, I'd just been put in a spotlight that I didn't want at all.

"Glad you could join us, Ms. McFee," Principal Feathers said, not looking glad one bit.

"So as I was saying, who here has been a victim of bullying?" Feathers continued.

What an idiot. What kid who'd been bullied was going to stand up and admit it in front of the whole school?

Stand up and say, yeah, I had my lunch money stolen or my homework papers thrown on the ground or my clothes made fun of. Leave it to Feathers to deal with his bully problem in the worst possible way. Even Leo was staring straight ahead and not about to raise his hand.

When it was obvious that no one who really had been bullied was going to admit it, Feathers moved on.

"Well, we know that bullying sometimes occurs, so we have decided to start a 'No-Bully Team' that will be on the lookout for bullies and stop them in their tracks.

As of today, Hickory Hills Middle School is officially a No-Bully Zone."

He smiled, but no one smiled back, and then he looked like he expected us all to start applauding.

No one did.

Everyone just stared at him as he kept his fake smile plastered on.

Even a dummy like me knows that there was a lot more to ending bullying than saying, "It's not allowed." Seriously, Feathers, how clueless can you be?

His fake smile slipped a little bit, but he kept going. "Here to kick off our new program is a short video from the Center for Bully Prevention showing the painful consequences of bullying. Mrs. Schmidt, the video," he continued.

The theater went dark, and Principal Feathers moved off the stage as a video clip that looked about thirty years old began to play. The opening scene showed a single kid who was so small he must have been a third grader walking down a school hallway.

Out in the crowd I heard a loud whisper, "Hey, there's Leo!" Then more laughter.

In the video, a group of four boys surrounded the small boy. The bullies took him into a bathroom and pretended to give him a swirly. It looked so comical and obviously fake that no one could take it seriously, and everyone in the theater howled with laughter.

A film that was supposed to make us feel bad about kids being bullied was actually funnier than an Adam Sandler movie. Who thinks of this stuff, and why do adults think that they know how to reach kids?

The stupid clip went on another minute with the poor kid crying, and then a group of smiling kids with capes came in and saved him from the Swirly Monster. Kids were laughing out loud, and their reaction was definitely not what Feathers was going for.

The principal was so out of touch that he didn't realize that he'd already made the problem worse. His dumb video made it seem OK and funny to bully a kid.

How did he get the job of principal?

After the lights came back on, Principal Feathers took up the microphone again and told us to be quiet.

"And now, I'd like to introduce our newly formed BullyBusters squad that will be responsible for policing our halls and reporting any bullying to me."

He began reciting names, and the first one was Matthew Rice. Matthew lived in my neighborhood, and though he was a big jock, he wasn't mean like Colin. After that were a couple of other boys and girls I'd seen around school who seemed pretty nice, so I thought maybe Feathers had actually picked kids who could help.

That thought lasted ten seconds.

It took Feathers that long to get to the names of some of Colin's buddies, and they made their way onto the stage laughing and pushing one another. I knew then for sure that the whole program was going to be a joke and just Feathers' way of saying he was working on a problem, when in reality he wasn't.

As he read the names, the students walked up on stage and got a button to wear that said "Bullies" and had a big red slash through it. Yeah, a button is going to stop a bully for sure. Only if you can get close enough to poke an eye with the pin.

I tried to see Harper's reaction to all this when Principal Feathers said, "And now the Captain of our Bully-Busters, Colin Markus."

There was a second of stunned silence as the idea that the cruelest boy in school could actually be in an anti-bullying group AND be its Captain sank in. Surely there was a mistake. Surely Ms. McFee would tell Feathers what a terrible idea it was to have Colin on his team.

I could see kids whispering to one another, and when I looked at Leo, he sat slumped down in his chair while Bernie patted his arm and stared at the stage with an angry look on her face.

Colin strutted up to the stage and got his button, and his lame group of followers began clapping and yelling his name.

"Quiet. Quiet," Feathers told the crowd. "Now, as we're being dismissed back to class, I'll play our new No-Bully rap song written by our own school counselor, Mrs. Schmidt!"

A groan went through the place. Teacher raps were always stupid, and I was sure this would be another loser. The speakers crackled to life, and I could hear Mrs. Schmidt's nasal voice attempting to rap.

"Don't be a bully, don't you see
bullying hurts both you and me
being mean is bad being mean is cruel
being a bully makes you look like a fool
Fool fool fool...cruel cruel cruel"

The tape continued with some strange fake drum-beat, and then her voice came on again, rapping the same dopey lyrics with the same thumping beat.

So here was our school's answer to a real problem.

A joke of a video, a group of bullies on the no-bullying team, and a rotten rap.

We were doomed.

The crowd was making its way out of the theater and some kids were starting to make fun by rapping along with the tape. The clueless adults thought that the kids liked the rap, and Mrs. Schmidt smiled and clapped her hands — out of time with the beat — and Feathers stood to the side of the stage talking with a news reporter.

What a sham. As we filed past the stage, Colin came up and whispered something into Leo's ear. Leo went a little pale, but didn't say a word back to him.

Bernie stared hard at Colin, but he just lifted his badge to show her that he was on the principal's team now, and there wasn't much she could do about it. He was right, of course.

Who would believe that the leader of the Bully-Busters was actually the worst bully of all?

CHAPTER SIX

We were all silent as we filed back into class. No one wanted to say too much with McFee hovering around, but we all knew that Colin now had more power than before. Leo especially seemed kind of out of it, and even when we went back to social studies, his favorite subject, he'd just give one-word answers.

"So what did you think about our assembly?" asked McFee when she realized that her lesson on the Thirteen Colonies was bombing pretty badly.

"Same ol' sh...I mean stuff," Skeever corrected himself after a warning look from McFee. "A lot of talk. No real action," he went on. "Everyone knows that there are bullies here. Real bullies who do some pretty messed up things. But no one wants to step in and get rid of them."

That was a true statement if I'd ever heard one.

"Well, I can only report what you guys tell me," Ms. McFee said. "Unfortunately, I don't always see what really happens in the halls or on the buses, so I rely on students to give me information."

"But nothing happens when we tell," Xin blurted out, and then he looked around, embarrassed. "I mean, nothing happened when I told last year. Feathers just wrote names down, talked to them, and then they made it even worse for me because I told. Why do you think I ride my bike to school every day? Even in the rain? Cause I can't ride the bus with those jerks anymore."

"Look, I've only been here two weeks," Bernie added. "And even I know that Colin kid's bad news. But Feather Brain gives him the No-Bully Crown? That's just messed up."

"Are you sure Colin's bad news?" Ms. McFee asked nervously.

I think that we all gave her such a look of disgust that she couldn't help but get our message. Of course he's bad news. And of course he always had been.

Colin's family had tons of money, and Mr. Markus was some kind of local politician who decided the school board budget and made big donations every year. Every principal I've ever had practically wiped Colin's butt for him. No one stopped him because they were afraid of the consequences if they had to deal with his dad.

I guess that made his dad a bully, too.

"Ms. McFee, Colin's not really that bad," Leo said in a quiet voice.

Now he was getting the are-you-crazy stare from all of us.

Not that bad??

Was Leo nuts?

Leo who got teased practically every day? Leo who could've been the boy in the stupid no-bully video who got his head pushed in a toilet? Leo who couldn't take a step out of this classroom without being afraid of his own shadow?

Not that bad? Leo had obviously snapped.

"And bullying really isn't so much of a problem here at school," he went on. "Can we go back to talking about the colonies, please?"

The rest of us looked at one another in stunned silence. If the kid who got bullied every day didn't want to admit that there was a problem, then what were we supposed to do about it? Weird stuff.

When Ms. McFee sent us for our early lunch, I saw Bernie talking closely in Leo's ear, and he even smiled a tiny smile as they trooped down the hall. I followed close behind with everybody else. Harper had started sitting by me when we had lunch in the classroom, so I didn't want to get too far from her in case it was just a coincidence.

I realized that I'd not made too much progress with Harper in the two weeks we'd been in school together. Even though I'd Googled pick-up lines ("Did the sun come out or did you just smile?" or "If I could rearrange the alphabet, I'd put U and I together"), I'd never got up the nerve to say one to Harper. I just kept helping her with math and trying to keep food out of my braces when we ate our lunch.

As we walked past the theater on the way to the cafeteria, the Anti-Bully Boneheads came pushing and laughing their way out of the auditorium. Colin stopped when he saw Harper, and I saw him look at his friends and nod his head. They all spread out in a line and we couldn't get past.

"Hey beautiful, do I know you? Cause you look a lot like my next girlfriend," Colin said to Harper as his friends all exchanged high fives and loud laughs.

"Good one, Colin!" Goon Number One said.

Wait! That was number twelve on my pick-up line website! Colin stole my line!

"No. We've never met," Harper instantly answered. "And honestly, after what I've just heard about you, I think I'll take a pass."

Colin's friends laughed even louder at that, and Harper turned to me.

"Come on, Jack. Let's get lunch," and she pushed through the line of boys with an "excuse me," and they moved out of her way. The rest of us followed behind her.

If Colin was embarrassed by Harper's diss, he didn't show it.

"Sure. Go get your lunch and get back to your closet class. Why would I want to go out with a stupid SPED-head like you, anyway?" Colin yelled as we walked away.

Ahead of us, Bernie stopped in the hall, and I could see Leo holding her back. Neither Xin nor Skeever looked surprised, and both just kept walking, as did Bryce. We'd all heard this garbage before, though I wondered when the SPED insults would stop stinging.

Principal Feathers came out of the auditorium as our group walked away. He had to have heard every word that Colin had just yelled, but he just told the boys to "get a move on," and walked past without giving us a glance.

So an hour after his anti-bullying rally, and Feathers walked right by real bullying in his halls? There would be no help from him.

We spent our days isolated in a tiny classroom and didn't take his precious tests to keep his school top-ranked, so the SPED kids didn't exist in his school or his world.

Not to mention my dad only sold paint and didn't have the power to run Feathers out of a job like Colin's dad could. The deck was stacked way against us.

Colin and his boys did what the principal told them and walked the other way, but Colin couldn't resist one last comment. "I see they let the monkeys out of their cages early today, guys...oooohhhh ooooohhhhh oooohhhh," he sounded as he hopped around scratching his pits.

"I wouldn't be putting my hands in those arm-pits...especially if you're gonna use them to eat," Bernie yelled from our end of the hallway.

She just didn't let up. Outnumbered and definitely out-muscled, this skinny little girl had a mouth on her that wouldn't stop. I wondered how she got so brave. I also wondered if maybe she could teach me a thing or two.

We all moved through the cafeteria line thinking our own thoughts when I saw Bryce shaking his head slowly as we picked up our fruit cocktail. "What's up, Bryce, don't like the lunch today?" I asked as we slid our lunch trays down the counter top towards the lunch lady and her cash register.

He looked at me squarely in the eyes and shook his head again. "Not right," was all he said, and then he went back to paying for his three of everything on the lunch line.

Part of me wanted to think he was referring to the mystery meat that they were serving for lunch again, but the honest part of me knew he was talking about how the SPED kids were treated here at HHMS.

CHAPTER SEVEN

After lunch, the day progressed normally with Boring Math followed by Kind of Interesting Science followed by Always Awful Grammar. I mean, seriously, who cares if you need an object pronoun or a subject one? Today's lame worksheet said, "Pass *me or I* the salt." *Me or I??* Really? Just pick a pronoun already and pass the stupid salt.

The afternoon announcements finally came on, and we breathed a sigh of relief. Today had been another routine Friday except for the new BullyBusters and the fact that we all wondered why Leo had defended Colin. Why hadn't Leo told Ms. McFee the truth?

As the announcements went on and on, we were all anxious to get out the door for the weekend, and Feathers was the last thing standing between us and freedom. Or was it we and freedom? Again, who cares, just get we *and* us outta here!

Like an annoying car alarm that just wouldn't stop, Feathers' voice could be heard through the static on the speaker.

"Students. I hope that everyone will join me as we work to make our school a Bully-Free Zone."

No one even looked up when he said it. We'd said as much as we could about that, and honestly it was too depressing to think about.

"Also, I want to announce that it's time for our annual Fall Festival. This year, thanks to a generous donation from Mr. Markus, we're going to be fortunate enough to have a professional DJ come to entertain at the dance."

That got our attention. They used to have a dance here at HHMS years ago when we were in elementary school, and all the older kids loved it. But when Feathers became principal, he thought he should choose the music *and* be the DJ, so the dance got so dull no one went anymore. Something about hearing "YMCA" for the two-hundred-zillionth time made kids just want to stay home.

Of course, it was Colin's dad paying for the DJ, so that meant Colin would be bragging even more than usual, but a dance might be my chance to spend some time outside of SPED-land with Harper.

"Hey, Leo. A dance, huh?" Bernie said as we waited for the final dismissal to the buses. "You gotta come bust a move with me. We'll show these folks how it's done."

Leo smiled his sad smile. "Aw, Bernie. I can't dance."

"No really, Leo. We should all go as a group. It'll be fun," Harper added.

Xinho and Skeever exchanged high fives. "Hella yeah," said Xinho. "Everyone knows that Asians are the best dancers."

A group? Wait a minute. There went my alone time with Harper. Though who was I kidding. Even if I did have alone time with her, I doubt if I could get the nerve to say much.

We finally heard the dismissal, and everyone began to head out. Usually I went to the buses with Leo and Skeever and everyone, but today my mom was getting me for an orthodontist appointment. I was going out to the front of the school with the car riders and students who walked or rode bikes to school.

I tried to walk closely behind Xin and Harper, but I didn't want them to think I was following them. Harper turned her head and saw me, though.

"Hey, Jack. No bus today?"

"No. My mom's getting me."

"Same here. My mom gets me every day, though. She won't let me ride the bus."

"Lucky. The bus sucks," I told them.

"Beyond sucks, dude. It is a rolling torture chamber," Xin agreed.

"But at least I'd meet people on the bus," Harper said. "I mean I come in, go to SGS, and then leave. You guys are super nice and all, but I don't really have any friends."

Xin looked offended. "I consider you my friend."

"Well, sure, but we don't hang out after school or go to movies or anything. I mean friends who do stuff together."

"Oh. That kind of friend," Xinho said.

She laughed. "Yeah, that kind. It's going to be a long year here if I never meet anyone."

As we were walking, I saw Britney and her clique laughing and shrieking down the hallway. They had changed into their cheer outfits and were swishing away with their pompoms. They acted like being cheerleaders made them better than anyone else, and I veered towards the other side of the hall.

Harper didn't. She went straight for them before I could warn her, and Xin and I stopped in our tracks to watch.

"Hi! Great pompoms!" she said brightly.

The crew stopped and looked immediately to their leader to see how to react. Were they so dumb that they didn't *know* what to do on their own or did they just have to stay in line to avoid being her target?

"Um. Thanks," Britney said as she looked at Harper and totally ignored Xinho and me.

"Yeah, I used to cheer in California, but I came here too late to try out," Harper told them.

She was a CHEERLEADER? I had a crush on a CHEERLEADER? What an idiot I was.

She'd never in a million years look at a lowly SPED-head like me. I didn't even play sports on video games, much less in real life. Walking was about as active as I got, and I had a tendency to trip over my own feet.

"Really? How long have you been cheering?" Queen Mean asked Harper.

"Oh gosh. Forever. My brother's a lot older than me, and he played football so I started young. I was one of the little girls who ran around the sidelines waving a banner and drooling on everything. I actually miss it a lot."

Britney looked Harper up and down, and she must have decided then and there to let Harper in the Circle of Phonies because she gave a nod to her girls and a tight smile of acceptance to Harper.

"Cool. You can come watch us practice sometime and maybe teach us some California tricks," Britney said.

"Wow. That would be great," Harper said. "Here's my number. Just text me and let me know when you guys practice."

Xin and I stood there like lurches while Harper rattled off her number, and it was all I could do not to write it on my hand. I think I remembered the first five numbers anyway. I'd write them down when I got in my mom's car.

Though since I didn't have a cell phone, what did it matter?

The cell business done, the other cheerleaders stood behind Britney, and I could see two of them whispering and staring at Xin and me. That made me mad and embarrassed at the same time.

"Well, I gotta go," Harper said. "My mom is waiting for me in the carpool line."

"Yeah, we have to go, too. Practice starts in five minutes." Britney said and turned to leave.

"See you at practice sometime!" Harper yelled as they walked away.

Britney didn't respond but just lifted her chin to show she'd heard. The Über Cool Chin Lift was apparently the latest and greatest way to communicate among the Popular Crowd. I always saw the jocks doing it to one another in the hall. One lifted his head and said "'sup." Roughly translated that means, "What's up?" and the other lifted his chin to show that he heard and that everything was up.

It looked like a nervous tic to me, and I thought I'd stick to waving.

As the girls pranced and giggled down the hall, I swore I heard the word SPED loud and clear followed by a burst of laughter. Of course, they couldn't resist a dig at us. I sure hoped that Harper knew what she was getting into with that crowd.

"Sweet. I'd just told you guys that I needed some friends. And then there they were! Perfect timing!" Harper said, practically jumping up and down in excitement. Xin and I just looked at one another but didn't say a word to Harper about the downside of her new "friends."

We got to the carpool line, and Harper waved to her mom who had just pulled up. Of course she had a Hot Mom (not surprising) and who drove a Badass Mercedes (again not surprising). Harper jumped in the front seat and waved goodbye to Xin and me.

Xinho said "See ya," and unlocked his bike from the rack and began his ride home.

I was left alone to wait for my Not Hot Mom and our Uncool Minivan and think about what had just happened.

Harper was so excited about meeting Britney that I didn't want to tell her that her new friend ate her old friends for breakfast. I also didn't want to tell her that Britney and Colin were tight, and once she heard that Harper had dissed him, she probably would take back her offer of cheer coaching and start a hate campaign against Harper like she had Anna.

Not my business. Not my fight.

I'd used that policy to get through two years of middle school, and it had worked just fine. No reason to change now...was there?

CHAPTER EIGHT

So the ortho told me to expect at least another six months in braces, but that I should be glad I wouldn't have to wear them to high school.

I was glad to hear they'd be off before high school, but I wondered if Doctor TortureMouth had ever had metal wires in his head to worry about. Looking at his crooked teeth, I decided that he'd never had braces. I think McFee would call that irony, which is something we'd learned about in English. I would try and remember to ask her on Monday.

After we left the orthodontist's office, my mom said we'd pick up dinner somewhere and then go rent a movie. This had been the Friday Night Plan for as long as I could remember. Take-out food and a corny kids' movie. While it had been fine in elementary school, I'd just kind of tolerated it in sixth and seventh grade.

Now that I was in eighth grade, I was starting to feel kind of embarrassed to always hang out with my parents on Friday nights.

Maybe I needed some friends, too.

My mom called in our order for an extra large pizza with black and green olives – we're crazy like that – though of course she had to get whole-wheat crust and low fat mozzarella. I'm sure the pizza guys used whatever they wanted on our order, but it made her feel better to at least try to get a healthy pizza. While they were making our pie, we walked into the video store next door.

I was reading all the new release titles when I heard my mom from across the store.

"Hey, Jack. Have you seen this? It looks fun," my mom asked holding up the latest SpyBratz movie.

Some kids in the store looked up at her waving the DVD box over her head and laughed. Jeez. Why did I have to have the World's Most Embarrassing Mom?

"Yeah, Mom, when I was about six," I answered, trying to sound like a punk kid.

"Oh, sorry," she said in a hurt voice. Great. Now I was hurting my mom's feelings because of random kids in a video store.

Feeling bad but not too bad, I walked over to her with a copy of *Lords of Fighting*, which was rated PG-13. Since I was 13, I figured what the heck.

Mom took the DVD case from me and read the back of it.

"Hmmm... it says rated PG-13 for language, violence, and sexual references. Sexy references!?" she practically shouted that last part and the Random Kids laughed again.

"Calm down, Mom. They have to put that on there. It's really not that bad. Xinho told me about it and said it was good." This was a bit of a stretch since Xin had only said he wanted to see *Lords of Fighting*, but I was desperate.

I was seriously tired of seeing only PG movies, and it was time to take a stand.

Right here.

In the Movie X-Change.

"I guess. But we're going to get *SpyBratz in Adventureland* as a backup. If there's something I don't approve of in this movie, off it goes," she said holding *Lords of Fighting* like it was a piece of smelly garbage.

"Deal," I answered, knowing that once I got Dad on my side, I could probably win this movie battle. Honestly, I'd just never tried before to watch something that she wouldn't approve of because it really didn't matter that much to me.

But now, after being laughed at in the assembly, made fun of at school for being in SPED, and now laughed at in the video store, it really did matter.

Hmmmm.

Maybe I was growing up.

Maybe this was the start of my Rebellious Phase.

I pictured myself wearing all black and listening to head banging music.

Then I pictured my mom storming into my room to turn down the music.

Maybe not.

We got our videos and went to pick up the pie, and my mom had to ask if it was low fat cheese and stone ground organic wheat flour. They automatically said yes, though I saw one guy wink at the other pizza guy and laugh. Obviously my whole family was doomed to be laughed at. I guess it's genetic.

After the short drive home, we met my dad in the kitchen, and he put up his hand for a high five. Instead I gave him the Cool Chin Lift and said "'sup." He stood there with his hand out and gave me a confused look.

"Sup? You mean supper?"

"No, Dad," I sighed. "'sup means 'what's up?' though you have to lift your chin when you say it."

"Ahhhh. I get it now." And he jerked his head up like someone was pulling his hair from behind and smiled. "'sup, my brother," he added with a bizarre raising of his eyebrows and a weird flapping of his elbows.

Yup. It's genetic all right.

"How was school?" Dad asked as he helped himself to a piece of pie.

"Just OK. Principal Feathers has started this lame anti-bullying routine."

"That sounds like a very worthwhile idea. Bullying is a big problem nowadays," my mom said as she handed my dad a plate.

"It's always been a big problem, Sofie," Dad said.

"Tom, you know what I mean. It's in the news a lot more now. People take it more seriously than when we were kids."

"Yeah. Rocco Spinelli put my head in the toilet a dozen times when I was growing up, and no one did much more than pass me a towel," Dad said between bites.

Ouch. Here was proof positive that my problems were inherited. Oh well.

"Rocco Spinelli? He seemed like such a nice boy!"

Hey, could we come back to the present, please folks?

"Sure, it's a problem," I said, interrupting their hike in Memory Valley. "And to make it worse, Feathers put the biggest bully of all as the leader of the Anti-Bullying team."

"What? I can't believe he'd do a thing like that," my mom said.

"Mom. He doesn't know everything like you think he does. He's a clueless idiot who has no business being in charge of hamsters, much less kids."

"Jack. That's so disrespectful. Principal Feathers is a professional educator who knows how to run a school. I can't believe you'd talk like that about an adult," my mom answered.

"Well I can't believe you'd take his side over mine. Again!!" I tossed my half-eaten pizza down and started to my room.

"Again? What's he talking about?" I heard her say as I was leaving the kitchen.

She obviously didn't remember me asking her to get me out of SGS and her going along with Feathers to keep me in.

"Who knows, hon. He's a teenager. We gotta remember that and roll with the punches," I heard Dad say with a mouthful of pizza.

"I'd like to roll him," Mom said as I was stomping up the stairs. "Down the driveway!"

Now I understood why so many teens complained that their parents didn't understand them. They didn't. I usually tried to go along and get along, but sometimes you just had to go *against* the flow. Mom thought that she and Feathers knew what was best for me, but I had to make her see she was wrong. No way was I spending the next four years in SPED-land.

Once I got in my room, I realized that I didn't eat my pizza, there was nothing to do, and it was only 6:17 on a Friday night.

Sigh.

I really did need to get some friends.

I was reading a book and trying to decide how long I should stay in my room to punish them and prove that I was the victim when I heard a knock on my door.

"Hey JackAlack. Can I come in?" my dad asked, even though he was already in.

"Sure, Dad. But no lectures on respecting authority or going along to get along," I told him up front. Those were my mom's favorite subjects whenever I tried to disagree with her.

"Absolutely. I hear you, son. You're getting older and getting your own opinions, and that's tough on your mom. To her, you're still a little guy who needs her to cut his meat."

Actually, I sometimes would love some help when she serves those big pork chops, but I kept quiet about that.

"Dad, she really doesn't get it about Feathers. The guy's a danger to our school."

"Jackster. That seems a bit exaggerated. He can't be that bad," Dad said leaning back on my bed.

"He's worse. He's blind to how mean some kids are. Dammit Dad, he made the biggest bully at our school the captain of the BullyBusters!"

"Whoa, son. Language check."

"Dad! And he's the reason we're locked up in a tiny closet learning all by ourselves."

"I can see you're really worked up about this, and honestly I'll have to think through how to help. He's the principal, you know, and running the school is his job...he should know what he's doing," Dad said as he got up to go. "Listen, JackMcSlack, why don't you come down and we'll watch the PG-13 movie...even if there are sexy references in it!" he added with a wink.

Sigh. He was trying to be on my side in the SPED battle, but he still didn't get it. I'd realized that this problem wasn't like falling on the playground or not understanding a science question.

Some things a kid just has to figure out on his own.

CHAPTER NINE

The weekend progressed like they all did, with movie night on Friday, helping out some at my parents' store during the day on Saturday, and being bored out of my mind on Saturday night. On Sundays, the paint store was closed, so my mom did all her errands and cleaned the house and junk like that.

Dad and I tried to stay out of her way and watched football or something on TV, but sometimes she made me come grocery shopping with her and it was the worst. Watching my mom take fifteen minutes to decide on which low-fat yogurt to buy would crush anyone's spirit.

I guess this Spending the Entire Weekend with My Parents was another thing that I'd have to go against the flow on pretty soon.

My mom didn't know what she was in for.

At school on Monday, we all filed in half asleep and quiet, the regular Monday March, except today there was no Bernie. She hadn't missed one day of school since we started, so it was kind of weird not to have her funny comments and observations about how bad we all smelled.

After the announcements were finally over, no one spoke for a minute as we adjusted to Monday.

"Hey, Ms. McFee," Leo piped up, "do you know where Bernie is?"

"She'll be a little late this morning, Leo. But she's fine."

Harper had her head down, and I noticed her trying to text under her desk.

Uh-oh. Didn't she know that McFee would put her phone in the "Drawer of Darkness" if she was caught? The Drawer was where McFee put anything she took from kids when they were messing around instead of paying attention. Leo had lost books, Xin had lost his iTouch, I even lost my favorite whoopee cushion last year.

I used to be so immature.

If she caught you with something while she was trying to teach, she took it and put it in the Drawer for a month. No exceptions. Even Bryce lost his Pokemon cards once, and I thought we were all going to die.

I tried to catch Harper's eye and get her to put the phone away, but she was too involved in her texts. Since I couldn't get Harper to pay attention to me, I decided to get McFee's attention instead just as she was saying for us to "Get out your science books..."

"Um, Ms. McFee, can I ask you something before we start on science?" I said.

"Can't it wait til later, Jack?"

"No. It's pretty important. So, can we step outside a minute?"

"I guess, Jack. Quickly though."

As we were walking outside I bent down to Xin and said, "Tell Harper about the Drawer."

He got it, and I could see him leaning over to whisper to Harper as McFee and I stood outside.

"So what is it, Jack?"

Good question. What was it??

Thinking fast, I remembered that we still needed to talk about my high school classes, and now seemed like as good a time as any.

"Well, I just want to know why I can't get out of SGS for high school. You know. Be in regular classes," I asked her.

"Jack, actually, I'd been meaning to talk to you about something," McFee began with a super serious look on her face that made me a little nervous.

"You mentioned on the first day of school that you wanted to be a forensic scientist, but honestly, I don't know if that's going to work for you," she finished.

I just stared at her wondering how we got from Harper and her phone to me and my future.

"I've checked, and you need a college degree for that kind of job, and to get to college you need a certain track in high school..." she went on.

"So put me in that track," I said.

"Well, I've checked that too, and unless you're in regular classes – not small group – in middle school, then there aren't regular classes for high school either."

This wasn't at all what I'd been expecting when I brought her outside, so I just looked at her and tried to follow what she was telling me.

"What do you mean?" I said.

"I guess what I mean is that since we don't offer regular classes for kids with your disability, you won't be able to get a college track diploma."

Disability!?! I hated that word. It made me sound like a handicapped veteran you'd see in a wheelchair outside of the bus station.

"I'm sorry, Jack," she continued and looked sadly at me.

"But Harper said she was in classes at her old school that had a regular teacher and a SPED teacher. They did that in my elementary school too, so why can't they do that here?"

"Well, since Hickory Hills Middle doesn't offer that type of program, the high school doesn't offer it either. Once you get to high school, it's either college track or SGS, and there's nothing in the middle," she said.

"But why don't we have it here? Why can't we be in regular classes and just get extra help?"

"It's not my decision, Jack, and I don't agree with it, but that's just not the way it's done here," she answered.

"Well maybe it should be!" I was getting pretty worked up. What had started as a distraction to keep Harper's phone out of the Drawer had actually gotten important.

"Jack. I understand you wanting to get out of SGS, but honestly, I think you should trust that Principal Feathers and the school system know what's best for you."

I stared at her in shock. This was the teacher who always said we could be who we wanted. Do what we wanted. And now she was holding us back?

"Wow, Ms. McFee. I guess it's good to know who's on my side in this."

"Now, Jack," she began, but was cut off as Bernie came scowling around the corner.

"Bernie! There you are! How did it go?"

Bernie just stared at her.

"Well? What happened?"

"What do you think happened? Another family says I got to leave. Another place that doesn't want me. Another social worker who doesn't care where I end up. What happened is what always happens. I got this month, and then I'm gone."

She turned and walked into the room.

"Jack. I'm sorry I don't have the answers you want, but I need to see about Bernie."

"Sure," I said as she went back into the classroom.

Wow. I couldn't imagine what Bernie must be feeling. To know that you have to leave, to go to where? I thought again about all the junk she'd been through. New schools all the time. New houses and no place to call her own.

I went back into the room feeling kind of stupid for complaining about my stuff when Bernie's stuff was much bigger. She'd obviously told the class because everyone was standing around her desk. Leo looked like he was going to cry, and Harper had put her phone up and was hugging Bernie.

"Same old stuff," Bernie said (though she didn't say stuff) as she slumped down in her desk. "Don't even try to tell me not to cuss, Ms. McFee," she went on without looking up.

McFee just looked at Bernie with a sad expression on her face and nodded. Then she let out a big sigh and quietly said, "Turn to page 211 in the science book, please."

We all did as she asked, but our minds were on anything but science.

CHAPTER TEN

At lunch Leo and Bernie were huddled in the corner talking quietly while Xin and Bryce were eating and playing a computer game. Skeever never ate of course, so he was reading a book while McFee answered emails.

That left Harper and me to entertain ourselves during lunch. I was glad that the cafeteria hadn't served anything with spinach or lettuce in it. Green slime in braces wasn't a good look on anyone, and I definitely wanted to talk to Harper while we ate. She needed to be warned about the Drawer, and I wanted to know who she was so interested in texting.

"How was your weekend?" I casually said as I bit into today's Lame Lunch.

"It was good. My mom took me to the mall, and my brother came home from college for the weekend."

"Cool."

Awkward Pause.

"Um. Is that who you were texting in class?"

"Oh! No!" she laughed and took big bite of her sandwich. She didn't have braces, of course, so she didn't worry about green slime getting caught in them.

"I was texting Britney. She's in Cressly's class, and that lady's blind. She never sees kids on their phones."

"Well, Cressly may be blind, but McFee isn't. If she sees you texting, your phone'll go straight into the Drawer of Darkness."

"Yeah. Xinho told me about the Drawer. Too funny! Britney had some stuff to tell me, so I thought I'd risk it."

Britney? Ugh. Anyone but her. How could I tell Harper that Britney might seem nice on the surface, but underneath she was pure evil? Did I give her the details about the time I'd once seen Britney untie the drawstring on Cassie Sinkwell's skirt so that when she stood up, the skirt dropped to the floor and Cassie was left standing in the library in her (flowered) underwear?

Harper wouldn't believe me or would think it couldn't happen to her. But I had to try.

"Britney Starks? The cheerleader?"

"Mm-hmm. She's been so nice to me. I think we're going to hang out next weekend."

"Harper. You might want to know that Britney isn't such a nice girl. She's done some pretty mean stuff to kids over the years."

"You know, Jack. You always seem to be warning me about anyone who isn't in SGS. You said that Colin was mean..."

"But you heard what he said to us last week after the assembly!"

"Britney said he was only joking. She said he's really nice."

NICE! The cruelest kid I'd ever met was NICE? Harper was kidding herself. How could she even start to believe that Colin was anywhere near nice?

"That's crazy. He's a jerk. You see what he does to Leo," I tried again.

"Actually, I have never actually *seen* him do anything to Leo. You just told me that he did stuff."

"Wow."

"Jack. You might be OK with having only six people in your life all day every day, but if I'm going to live here, I have to branch out. Britney's super popular, so if she wants to hang out with me, I'm going to at least try and be her friend."

"Wow."

"Stop saying that, Jack. You sound like somebody from *That '70s Show*!" she said, and I shut my mouth in a hurry. "Look, I have to have friends. People to talk to. You might like your situation, but I prefer friends under the age of forty who I don't call Mom or Dad."

Ouch.

That one stung.

How could she know that I spent every weekend with my parents?

Lucky guess, I supposed.

I could understand her wanting to have friends here in town, and new people were fine. But new people named Britney and Colin were a disaster. How could I make Harper understand?

"OK. I didn't want to tell you the gory details, but I guess I have to. In sixth grade, there was a new girl, a pretty new girl named Anna, who was a cheerleader and she became Britney's friend."

"Yeah. So?"

"Yeah, so, when people started liking her more than they liked Britney or giving her more attention or whatever it is people like Britney need, Britney and her group of witches started an all out war on Anna. They wrote mean stuff in the bathroom, they called her house all the time, they even sabotaged her cheer stuff and she almost broke her leg at a football game."

Harper stared at me, and I could tell she didn't believe a word of it.

"I can't see it. Britney and her friends might be a little catty, but they're nothing like what you're saying. I just think you don't want me to have anybody to talk to but you."

"What?" Uh-oh. How did she find me out?

"Seriously," she went on. "I can totally tell when a boy likes me, and you do. And I also can tell that even though you like me, you're too scared to do anything about it."

I sat there in shock and wondered whose bright idea it was to bring girls into SPED-land in the first place. I wished we had a fire alarm or something to get me out of this. My embarrassment must have shown on my face, because Harper tried to go a little easier on me.

"Look, Jack," she said, putting her hand on my arm. "You're a sweet guy, but your idea of fun is hanging out with your parents all weekend, you're content to be in a class with only six other kids, and you're in eighth grade and don't even have a cell phone." She stood up and started walking towards the door.

"I'm not one to judge," she finished as she threw away her lunch trash and totally prepared to pass judgment. "But all of that put together makes you seem kind of, well, lame." With that last dig, she left the room to go down the hall to the bathroom.

No one seemed to be paying us much attention, or maybe they just knew I was already suffering and didn't want to add to my plate of shame, so I sat there stunned.

Her comments were ringing in my ears, and when she listed it out like that, (my only friends are my parents, I know just six kids in a school of six hundred, and I don't have a cell phone) it *did* seem kind of lame.

But the question was, what could I do about it?

CHAPTER ELEVEN

When Harper came back from the bathroom, she apologized immediately and said that she didn't mean to hurt my feelings. But the fact that she'd delivered the news of my lameness in such a matter-of-fact way, without yelling or anything, was rough.

Those weren't words she'd said because we were arguing or fighting; they were words she'd been thinking for a while and they were true. I was lame.

The L on my forehead (Lame? Loser? Laughingstock?) was not only a capital letter, but blazing neon and blinking a mile a minute. I couldn't remember ever feeling much worse.

Later that afternoon, I sat at my desk and tried to listen to McFee talk about perfect squares and prime numbers, but I just kept replaying Harper's words in my head. I knew she was right, but I wasn't sure what to do about it.

How did you grow up? How did you make the move from a life filled with hanging with your parents to one hanging with your friends? Especially when you (don't tell anyone) didn't really mind your parents and FridayNight MovieNight all that much. At least when the movies were decent and the takeout was good.

Jeez. I wish I'd known getting older was so hard. I'd have stayed in kindergarten.

I snapped back to reality when McFee asked me a question about prime numbers, and I left my thoughts of lameness and growing up behind while I worked on math for a solid hour.

After that, the day was nearly over, and we all spent the last few minutes before the announcements talking about Bernie's news from this morning.

"I knew it was coming because it always comes," Bernie said with her chin in her hand. "I just wished they had waited longer than five minutes to send me packing."

"But isn't there another family here in town that could take you?" Harper asked. "Maybe you could live with me and my mom?"

"Girl. You're nice. But you're crazy. The courts hardly ever let a foster kid go where they want...they just put us where the next slot is open. I feel like a coin that goes in the vending machine but keeps getting spit out cause something's wrong with it."

"Stop saying that," Leo said from behind his book. "There's nothing wrong with you. What's wrong is a system that has a kid going to thirty-three schools before they're fourteen."

"Word," Xinho chimed in. "We gotta fight the system, man, we gotta fight the power," as he said this last part he raised a clenched fist and we all did the same.

Ms. McFee looked around at our raised fists and she could see that we were getting riled up. I think talking about "fighting the system" made her think of our argument this morning since she stood up and gave us all a hard look.

"No, Xin. No fighting the power. You have to work *within* the system because it's so big and powerful. Fighting it's a waste of time and effort."

This from the lady who wore Doc Martens to school and basically did what she wanted in here. Weird.

"I know you're all feeling for Bernie. I am, too, and I hate to think she might not be with us," McFee finished.

"There ain't a 'might,' Ms. McBee. I'm leaving," Bernie interrupted flatly.

McFee went stubbornly on, "but we have to work with the system the way it is."

"Not to contradict you, Ms. McFee," Leo said quietly, "but weren't we just talking about the Revolutionary War and how the Patriots decided King George's 'system' wasn't fair to them? Didn't the United States get created because some people fought the system?"

Got her there! Go Leo!

Before McFee could collect her thoughts and respond, Feathers' nasally whine came over the loudspeaker. She was saved by The Tool.

"Good afternoon Hickory Hills Middle School. Prepare for dismissal."

"That was different, Leo. Promise me no fighting anyone or anything. Got it?" McFee said as we collected our books.

She didn't realize it, but McFee was talking about more than just one fight. There was my fight to get out of SGS and become Not-As-LameJack. Bernie's fight against a system that treated her like a pinball instead of a kid and had bounced her around her whole life. And Harper who didn't even realize that she might have to fight to keep from getting chewed up and spit out by Britney and her Bunch.

It looked like LameJack may be *forced* to fight, and NewJack better come out swinging.

CHAPTER TWELVE

The first thing I did when I got home was go online and start looking at phones. I might not be able to get friends overnight, but I could definitely get a cell phone. My mom had always said I didn't need one because I never went anywhere (even she knew I was lame), but all that was going to change. Even if I had to go somewhere (backyard? down the street?) alone, I was going to start going somewhere other than to school and my house with occasional visits to the paint store.

NewJack was stepping out.

My dad had asked me before if I wanted a phone, but I never saw the need and I looked at a phone as just one more thing that would be tough to handle with dyslexia. People were always reading texts and stuff on their phones, and I didn't want the aggravation.

Until now.

This was one thing I could mark off Harper's List of Lame right away!

I started with the cell service that my parents had because I knew it'd be cheaper to just add a line to theirs. The website was amazing, and I couldn't believe all the phones and what they could do. It was like having the world in your hand.

Oh wait, that was their ad slogan.

Doing the research was actually fun as I looked at all the pictures of "cool" teens using their phones to text and call and play games. If getting a phone was all it took to get me out of LoserLand, then I was home free. Somehow I doubted it was that easy, but a kid could dream.

I narrowed it down pretty quickly to two models that weren't too expensive, printed out the information on both of them, and left them on the kitchen counter with the mail.

NewJack didn't waste time.

After thinking it through, I'd decided to go straight to Dad on this one. He was more concerned with my "social development" – I learned that from all my SPED paper-work – than my mom and would be easier to persuade. He was the one who wanted me to have friends and do stuff, while Mom was happy to keep me safe in a cocoon all the time, watching movies with her.

PG movies, of course.

Luckily for me, it was Mom's night to close the paint store, so Dad got home first and I went straight for the kill.

"Hey Dad, I think it's time I got a phone. I mean, how can I call or text my friends if I don't have my own cell?"

He was looking through the cabinet for a snack as I said this and stopped. "Really? You want a phone?"

"Yep. It's time."

"Great, JackSmack. Let's go to the store right now!"

"Now? I mean, we don't have to do it now…"

"Why not? I think it's great that you want a little independence and privacy. I mean, how can you talk to girls on the house phone? Your mom would be listening to every word!" Dad said as he grabbed his keys from the counter.

Jeez. He already had me talking to girls? My dad moved a lot faster than me.

"Um. I printed out some info on two phones that look good. Here," I said as I handed him the ads I'd found online.

"The Titan? No way, son. That's yesterday's technology. If we're going to get you a phone, let's get a PHONE!" When he shouted PHONE, he did it really loudly and put both fists up like he'd just won a race or something and began hopping around the kitchen.

The paint fumes at the store must be stronger than I thought.

"I'm thinking the FireX2000. That baby will do everything," he said when he calmed down.

"Dad, I think that one is kind of pricey. Mom might…"

He instantly cut me off and opened the door to leave. "Mom isn't here, Jack-a-Lack!! Come on, let's go before she gets home!"

Wow. I'd never seen my dad so excited about something. I guess he was tired of having LameJack around, too.

CHAPTER THIRTEEN

The drive to the phone store was a short one, and the whole way over my dad kept rattling off stuff about megs and rams and the four g's. Honestly, I didn't know he was so obsessed about phones, so I guess I didn't pay much attention after all. I knew he called on it, texted on it, got us directions to places on it, and sometimes watched a YouTube video on it, but I didn't know the dude had a college degree in cell phones.

The clerk knew him when we walked in the store, and that should've told me something right away.

"Hi, Mr. Parker," the smiling clerk said as he practically ran over to shake my dad's hand. "You can't be looking to trade in the SpitfireZX yet! That baby is state of the art!"

"Hey there, Jeff. No, not looking for me today. We're here to get JackSmack his first phone."

Of course he had to say "first phone" at top volume just as a kid who was probably eight shouted to his mom, "I want that phone, Mom." I saw the mom take one look at me, realize a life of Loserdom could be avoided for her child with the mere purchase of a phone, and she said, "I'll take it."

Sigh. Even third-graders were cooler than me.

"Awesome!" the clerk said in answer to my dad's announcement about getting me my first phone, and he raised his hand to give me a high five. I thought about doing the "sup" cool chin move but had already missed that chance. So I gave him a weak hand slap and tried to smile.

Dad had already taken off and was circling the store looking at all the models. He went immediately to the FireX model on display and handled it carefully.

"So this is the current model, Jack. It looks pretty good," Dad said to me as Jeff walked over.

"Looking at a FireX? Hold on just a minute, Mr. P. We got a shipment of NEW FireX's not twenty minutes ago, and I haven't even put them in inventory."

Dad's eyes lit up, "Not the new FireX3000?? It just came out two days ago...I didn't think you'd have any in stock."

"Mr. Parker...don't I always hook you up with the best stuff?"

"Don't toy with me, Jeffie...I might faint!"

If there was a NerdTown, I think my dad would be elected mayor. He was so into this phone stuff that I realized how hard it must have been for him to keep quiet as I traveled through life alone and phoneless. He'd probably wanted to get me a phone for as long as I'd been able to talk.

"Dad, I didn't know you were so into cell phones," I said as Jeff went to the back room.

"Yeah, I used to be a super computer geek when I was younger, before I got into the paint business," he answered.

"But how come you didn't push me to get a phone earlier if you're such a fan?"

"Everybody grows at a different pace, JackaLack. Besides, I didn't want to have a fight with your mother if *you* weren't asking for the phone yet. But once you asked...all bets were off!"

As we were talking, his eyes roamed the store like searchlights trying to see everything at once. He was even petting a fuzzy phone case as if it was a dog while we were talking. The man was obsessed!

"Cool. She's gonna be super mad, though," I said when I got his attention again.

"Nah. She knew it was coming. She's just trying to keep you out of the world a little longer. Moms are like that...or at least your mom is," he said.

"For sure. She'd love it if I still had naptime and used a sippie cup."

"Aww, she's not that bad. It's just hard to have your only child growing up and growing away."

"Is that why she won't let me out of SGS?" I asked.

"Now that I really don't know, son, but I haven't forgotten about checking on it," he answered just as Jeff brought out the FireX3000 in all its glory.

It was light and modern looking...no flip phone here. Dad said it was a touch screen, and I gave it a try and slipped my finger across the surface too fast to make anything happen.

"Weird," I said a little scared by its sleek look.

"Here's the best feature though," Jeff said, holding up the phone to his mouth.

"Call my mom," he said into the phone.

"You must program your mom's number in first," said the phone.

Wait, the PHONE talked back?

"YES!" My dad yelled. "It really is true! I read about this feature, JackSmack! My phone doesn't even have that! Too cool!"

I thought my dad had lost his mind if he imagined my mom going for a phone that could do all this crazy stuff. I mean, why did I need a *phone* I could talk to? Oh wait, maybe I needed it because I didn't have any real *friends* to talk to?

Maybe I could be the Mayor of LoserTown.

"This is nuts, Dad. We don't need to buy me such a fancy phone."

"Son, I want you to have this phone. I think you'll really like it. And I know the chicks will totally dig it! "

Now I knew he'd lost his mind. Phone or no phone, no "chick" was going to dig me. Not at least until I got these braces off and got the hell out of SGS. There was no point trying to argue with him, though, and I decided

that if he wanted to take the heat with Mom, then I'd
take the new phone. I could always just use it to play
video games on.

I left Dad to do the checkout part that would obviously take forever and started to walk around the store looking at other phones.

They finally called me over and Jeff was trying to teach me the basics on how to operate the cool little phone when I heard a familiar voice over my shoulder.

"Wow, Jack. You don't waste time, do you?"

My dad jumped in surprise when he heard a girl's voice talking to me, but I knew without turning around that it was Harper. She was there with her mom and stepdad, and we stood awkwardly for a minute til my dad the salesman jumped in.

"Hi there, I'm Tom Parker, Jack's dad," he said sticking his hand out.

"Hello, I'm Dara Finley, my husband Mark, and our daughter Harper."

"Ahhhh, the famous Harper I've heard so much about!?" I looked at my dad and thought about telling my phone to kill him.

But then he continued, "Just kidding. Jack never talks about anyone, so it's good to know he really does go to school with actual kids."

We all laughed at that, but Mrs. Finley piped up, "Well, a few kids anyway. I'm not sure I like the way they do special education here. Putting only the SPED kids together for the whole day and separating them from everyone else doesn't seem right to me."

"Uh-oh...don't get her started," Harper said. "She needs a mission and thinks it should be SGS. But I told her we don't even know how long I'll be here, so why bother?"

"Well, yes, you'll eventually be moving back to your dad's but what about the other kids in there?" Mrs. Finley said.

At that, all eyes were on me. I wanted to ask my phone to make me disappear, but instead I cleared my throat and said, "Yeah. I'm trying to talk to the teacher about it, but she won't really listen."

"Well, you let me know what I can do to help you, Jack," Mrs. Finley said.

"Mom!" Harper exclaimed and to me said, "she's always looking for a cause to help."

I think Mrs. Finley's offer to help offended my dad because he quickly said "Oh no, Mrs. Finley, we're absolutely talking to the school about Jack's placement for next year. Thanks for your offer, though."

Awkward much? I realized we needed to get home before Mom walked in to an empty house and called 911 to have them send over search dogs to find our bodies.

"Hey, Dad," I said turning to him. "We probably should go."

Jeff was still standing politely there during all of this. "So you good to go on the FireX3000, Mr. Jack?"

"Wait…what?" Harper stopped in her tracks. "So you go from no phone to the FireX3000??? Lucky!"

"Well, Jack's a busy kid, and I think this phone will help him stay organized," my dad said.

Busy? Me? Yeah, if you count how busy I'll be trying to learn to use this thing.

"Um, yeah, gotta stay organized, you know," I added.

"Awesome. I'm super jealous," Harper said turning around with a pleading look to her parents. "Hey, while we're here…"

They both said a loud "NO!" at the same time, and some customers jumped in surprise. That made us all laugh, and I wanted to leave before I did something embarrassing. Or before my dad spoke again which was the same thing.

"So, bye Harper. See you tomorrow," I said as we turned to go.

"Wait, Jack, don't you want to put my number in your phone?" Harper said with a smile.

Did I ever, but first I had to figure out how to turn it on!

With Jeff's help we programmed the phone and got Harper's number and my dad and mom's numbers in before we left the store. As we walked quickly to the car, I didn't say too much. I was trying to relive every word of the conversation with Harper and look for clues that maybe she didn't think I was still lame.

Maybe getting a phone took me out of lame category and up to loser? Or was loser worse than lame? I really didn't know unless you did it alphabetically, then lame came before loser.

"Let me handle your mom, Jack," my dad said on the way home. "And we don't have to mention the price if you know what I mean."

"Not a word from me, Dad. Thanks again. It's a really great phone," I told him.

"And it's already working! I saw how that Harper was staring at you!"

"Dad, if she was staring, it's because I had food in my braces. She told me at school today that I was lame."

"What? You're not lame!"

"And you're my dad, so of course you'd say that, but seriously, look at me."

He didn't say anything as we drove in silence.

"OK… I look at you and I see a nice-looking and polite kid with a great sense of humor, Jack. And a badass phone, of course," he said with a smile.

"Thanks Dad, but I see a kid who can't learn like other kids, who has no friends, and wears braces. With a badass phone, of course." I tried to smile so my dad wouldn't know how much it bothered me that I was a loser.

Luckily Mom still wasn't there when we got home. There must have been a run on paint and she couldn't close on time, so we were able to hide the big flashy box that the phone had come in. When she did get home, I was just going to let Dad do all the talking.

Besides, I had a phone I needed to learn to use.

CHAPTER FOURTEEN

I spent most of the night playing with my phone. Dad told Mom that he bought me a phone to use for "emergency purposes." Yeah, a nonexistent social life qualified as an emergency for sure.

After a lot of mess ups, I finally figured out how to go from the phone screen to the home screen, and I only cut off a conversation with my dad one time. I was practicing calling people, and he was my only number in the phone besides Harper's or my mom's. No way I was calling either of them.

When I got to school the next day, Harper was sitting there in the SGS room with a big grin on her face.

"So, I see that you're getting the hang of your new phone and that you had pork chops for dinner last night," she said as I was sitting down.

"Um. Yeah, I'm kind of figuring it out...but how do you know what I ate for dinner?" I prayed I didn't have pork chop breath. Gross.

"You did a butt dial around 6:30, and I got to hear your dad telling your mom a few choice fibs about how you needed a phone for 'emergency purposes,' and then he changed the subject to her yummy pork chops."

Oh jeez. How embarrassing!

"You mean I dialed you and didn't know it?"

"It's called a butt dial, brainiac. Or pocket dialing," Skeever chimed in. "Happens all the time. Or at least it happens to me all the time."

"How can it happen to you?" Xinho laughed. "You're too skinny to even have a butt!"

Please please please let me not have said anything too stupid while Harper was listening. She already thought I was lame, and I didn't want to know what came after lame...weird? Awkward? Gulp, hopeless?

"Jeez. I hope you didn't have to listen to my dad for too long," I said fishing a bit.

"No, once I realized you weren't really calling me, I hung up. Maybe next time we can try actually *talking* on the phone."

Next time? Did that mean she wanted me to call her or was she just being polite?

Girls were so tricky.

Bryce and Leo walked in from their buses, and it was then I realized that McFee wasn't here yet. She was sometimes late, so I didn't think too much about it. She knew that she could trust us on our own for a few minutes.

Just then someone opened our classroom door and walked in, and it definitely wasn't Ms. McFee.

Standing in the doorway was a little, shriveled-up old woman who looked like she belonged in an old folks home somewhere instead of a middle school.

"Goodness," she said, taking off her coat and sounding a little out of breath. "What a big building!"

We all just looked at her for a minute. Then Harper took over.

"Hi there, um are you lost or anything?"

"No, dear. I'm your substitute teacher. Filling in for a Ms. McBee."

We all laughed but quickly stopped so we wouldn't hurt her feelings. We didn't get subs often – McFee was a beast about coming to school and had come with colds and stitches and even an eye patch one time after a branch got her while she was Rollerblading.

"So, where's the rest of the class?" the sub said, looking around.

"Well, actually, we're only missing Bernie, so basically this is the class," Harper answered politely.

"Gracious. Only six of you? What about that...when I was a girl we had at least forty in a class."

"Yeah, crazy, right?" Harper said.

"So did they separate you because you're so much smarter than the rest?" the old lady asked.

Even Bryce laughed out loud at that one. Not hardly.

"No ma'am. The opposite actually. We're the school dummies. You know, this is the SPED room," I told her.

"SPED? You mean Speedy?"

Jeez she wasn't getting this...maybe she needed to be in SPED when she was younger.

Oops. Not nice.

"No...like Special Education...SPED for short."

"Oh. That's what that means! When I took the substitute job I saw 'special' and thought it meant you were special. And from the looks of you, I think it was right. Now let's see what your teacher left for us to do..."

We all looked at each other, and I thought about what she'd just said. I'd honestly never considered it that way. Seriously. I'd never seen the word "Special" as part of SPED. Maybe it didn't *have* to mean something bad. Maybe we really were special.

Just then Colin and his jerkface friends walked by and yelled into our room "Bite me, SPED HEADS..."

Or maybe not.

The day progressed pretty quickly. Bernie and Ms. McFee never showed up, which was strange, but we liked Mrs. Spriggins, our sub. She was chill and didn't mind when we did our homework in class or chatted while we did our assignments.

"My dears, this has been a lovely day," she said as we began making our end of the day movements and loading up backpacks. "And in my opinion, you're definitely a most special group."

Again with the "Special" label. I wondered when being in Special Ed had gone from something good to something terrible. How did that change?

"Weird about both McFee and Bernie being out on the same day. I hope they haven't taken Bernie early or anything and McFee was sad about it" Harper said.

"I doubt it. My dad always talks about how slow the government works," Xinho added. "So if they said she got to stay til the end of the month, she may even get an extra day or two."

"Yeah. I hate that she has to leave at all," Harper said.

"Me too," Leo added from his desk. "Colin and his creeps have actually been keeping their distance since she got here. I mean, that's not the only reason I want her to stay of course..."

"I know. You're friends and it's hard to lose friends. Believe me, I know all about that. I miss my girlfriends from California so much," Harper said.

This was a perfect opportunity to ask for a casual Britney update.

"But I thought you were becoming friends with Britney and her bunch," I asked, trying to appear totally uninterested since I didn't want to start a fight with Harper again.

"Oh, I am. We're hanging out next weekend. But it's not the same. I miss hangin' with my besties."

Just then Principal Feather's nasal tone came on for the afternoon announcements, and I was left to wonder exactly what teenagers did when they were "hangin' with besties."

"Thank you again, dears, for such a lovely day," Mrs. Spriggins said once the announcements were over. "So much better than yesterday with the kindergarteners over at Southlake Elementary. They were holy terrors!"

As she buttoned up her big coat, Mrs. Spriggins looked up at Bryce.

"Young man, could you possibly carry my bag to my car? It seems I'm just worn out after this long day."

Bryce didn't say anything about his bus being in the opposite direction of her car. He simply picked up her bag and stood by the door.

"Ah see, I was right. You're definitely very special children," Mrs. Spriggins said as she was leaving. "I certainly hope I get to sub for you again."

I thought about her view of us as being special all the way to my bus and wondered where the name came from in the first place. I guess they started calling it "Special Education" that so kids wouldn't feel badly for being different, but somehow over time it had become something so bad that we couldn't even be with regular kids anymore.

That's not too special.

I felt my phone vibrate with an incoming text and it startled me. I'd never gotten a text before!

Maybe it was from Harper!

Maybe she wanted to be Besties!

I looked down at my phone, and after a second to decode the words, I saw that the text was from my mom. "Hurry home. Chores waiting! Love Mom."

So much for Besties.

CHAPTER FIFTEEN

The next day at school we were all sleepily going through our morning motions. McFee was back and so was Bernie, but both looked angry and we all kept our distance. At the appointed hour, the speaker on the wall came to life and Principal Doofus started with the pledge, followed by an announcement that did get our interest.

"Tickets go on sale next week for the Fall Festival Dance. All students will want to attend this fun event complete with a DJ provided by the generous Mr. Markus."

"OK," Harper began. "Who's going with me?"

"You know I'll be there doing my Asian break dancing," Xin replied immediately.

"Definitely be there. A chance to run around the gym like a crazy person and not get detention? I'm in," Skeever said.

"What about you Leo, I hope you'll come," Harper said.

"Oh, I don't know...dancing doesn't sound like my thing," Leo said, not looking up from his book.

"But hanging out with your friends does, and I'm sure Bernie will be there, right Bernie?"

Bernie scowled up at us from her desk and gave a big sigh.

"IF I'm still livin' here, and IF I ain't busy, I might go to that stupid dance," she said. "But only because Leo needs someone to teach him to dance right."

Leo looked up from his dragon book, "Thanks Bernie. I'll have to ask my dad, though. He'll probably say no."

"So that leaves Bryce and Jack," Harper said looking over at both of us.

Just then McFee came up for air from her computer screen and barked at us. "Open your grammar book to page seventy-two and get busy," she said and then was back on her screen.

Grammar at 8:30 in the morning!?!

It was going to be a long day.

Fortunately McFee came to her senses by 9:15, and we started a normal lesson on some scientific something or other. She kept checking her email though and looking at her phone, so we all knew something was up.

I was trying to pay attention to the ins and outs of factoring equations as Ms. McFee wrote every step on the whiteboard when I saw Britney walk slowly past our door and stare in the little window.

Harper looked up, saw her, and jumped out of her seat. "Ms. McFee, can I go to the restroom?"

Without even turning around from her math problem, McFee said, "Harper, our break is not for another thirty minutes...can't it wait?"

McFee was a stickler for schedules.

"No, sorry, it's kind of an emergency," Harper answered.

"OK. Hurry back," McFee said and continued to work the math problem.

I knew Harper didn't have any emergency and that she was meeting Britney in the hall, but did I really care what they were up to?

I'd decided that I didn't care and was working the math problem with McFee when Harper waved at me from the little window in our door and gestured for me to follow her into the hall.

What? How weird was that. Why would Harper want me to follow her (and the Queen of Mean) to the bathroom? I decided to ignore Harper and focus on math, but she waved again from the door, and I was scared McFee or someone else would notice and Harper would get in trouble.

Seriously? What could she want?

Sigh. "Ms. McFee, um, can I go to the restroom? Definitely an emergency," I said, trying to look like I really had to go.

"What, too much OJ this morning, Jack?" Skeever said and everyone laughed.

I could tell McFee didn't believe me, but what teacher can say no to a kid standing in front of them doing the gottapee shuffle?

"Good grief. I guess we'll just take our break early," she said and put down her whiteboard marker.

Great. Now Harper would blame me for the SPED parade coming out while she was talking to Britney.

Everyone was giving me curious looks as we trooped into the hall, and I saw Harper and Britney quickly duck into the bathroom once they realized the whole class was coming out. Of course I had to go straight into the boys' room since that was the reason we were all out here. So I went in the bathroom and stared at the walls for a minute and read some new graffiti.

When I came out, Harper came out of the bathroom too and stood by me as I waited my turn at the water fountain.

"Jeez. I didn't say bring the whole class!" she said quietly.

"McFee told everyone to go when I asked."

"Oh. I just wanted to show Britney your phone."

"What? Why does she care about my phone?"

"I dunno. She said she wanted to see it."

"Well I'm not going to take it out in the hallway. McFee will see it and we aren't supposed to have phones on us...we're supposed to leave them in our lockers," I said getting a second drink of water.

"OK, OK, Mr. Rule Follower. I don't know why she wanted to see your phone anyway...I'd mentioned that I saw you in the phone store the other day, and she wanted to see your phone. Maybe she's going to get one," Harper said as we started walking back to class.

McFee came out of the faculty bathroom and began her shooing motions that meant it was time to head back in our room.

It made me nervous that Britney even knew I was alive much less was interested in my phone. I'd spent two peaceful years in the shadows here at HHMS, and I'd learned by watching others that having a girl like Britney pay attention to you could only be bad news.

I thought about trying to explain that to Harper but figured I'd sound like a freak.

I decided to keep quiet but stay on Mean Girl Alert.

Being scared to show Britney my phone would probably put me back in the "Lame" category and mess up any progress I'd made by getting a phone.

And people thought being a grownup was hard!

We all settled back in our desks, and I thought about the conversation after Feathers' dance announcement this morning. It looked like everyone was serious about going to the Fall Festival dance except Leo, who'd said he had to ask his dad, and maybe Bryce, who'd not said anything.

I knew that I wanted any opportunity to hang out with Harper, so I would go even though just saying the word "dance" made my armpits sweat a little.

Thinking it through, I realized that there was just one small problem with the whole dance idea.

The dancing part.

I'd been worried about this problem for a few days and had decided that who better to teach me to dance than our resident Asian Break Dancer?

Plus, I was also thinking that maybe if Xin and I hung out outside of school, we could qualify as friends and I'd come off of Harper's Lame Loser List.

Ahhhh, the joys of alliteration.

I approached Xin at lunch, sat down with my weird chicken-wannabe sandwich from the cafeteria, and looked hungrily at Xinho's sesame chicken with rice. It looked great and made my mystery meal look even worse by comparison.

"So what are you going to name your restaurant when you open it? Xin's Asian Palace of Fried Rice?"

"Nah. Gotta keep it simple. Thinking I'll call it Buddha's Belly or something like that."

"Awesome," I said starting to chew on my cardboard chicken.

"So, Xin, I was thinking," I continued, suddenly embarrassed to be asking for dance lessons.

"That's something new for you," Xinho joked.

"Funny, dude. But really," I began and lowered my voice in embarrassment. I definitely didn't want to advertise the fact that I couldn't dance and wanted to learn.

"I was kind of hoping that you could maybe teach me a few dance moves before the Fall Festival next week. I'd like to maybe ask Harper to dance, but I don't want to look like a SPED spaz if I do."

"No problem, my brother. I taught my cousin to dance before his sister's big Asian wedding. It was like a freakin Footloose convention at that party," he laughed.

"Sweet. You want to get together after school sometime?"

"Definitely, but the only day I'm not booked in tutoring or chess lessons or violin practice is Fridays."

"Violin?" I asked.

"I know, right? My parents are determined to make me into a typical brainiac violin-playing Asian, but I tell them that they are just wasting their money since I have zero talent," Xinho said.

"That's not true. You have talent, just look at your lunch! Fridays work for me, though. My usual Friday routine is takeout food and a movie with my parents."

"Wow. I thought I was lame," he laughed.

"No one's Friday night is as bad as mine," I agreed as we went to throw away our lunch trash.

I'd remember those words later in the week and decide that I was wrong.

Someone's Fridays were definitely way worse than mine.

CHAPTER SIXTEEN

The week went by quickly, and I waited until Thursday to tell my mom that I was going home with a friend on Friday. I figured that the later I told her about my plans, then the less time she'd have to consider it and say no.

As an added precaution, I planned on bringing it up around my dad. Since I knew he was all about me getting some friends, he'd definitely be on my side.

It was a normal Thursday night meal that consisted of (tofu) hot dogs and frozen (sweet potato) French fries. Why was my mom the health freak? Why couldn't she be a fanatic about something else like clean water or saving the whales?

I thought maybe next time Xin should come here and give her some cooking lessons that involved preparing real food.

We'd been talking about normal "how was your day" stuff when I decided it was time to tell them about going to Xin's. In preparation, I said a casual "Pass the mustard, please."

As my mom was passing the mustard, I added, "By the way, I'm going home from school with a friend tomorrow."

Both of my parents stopped eating and stared at me.

What a freak I must be if saying "I'm going home with a friend" stopped them both in mid-bite. Though come to think of it, the last time I went home with anyone was in third grade before I got put in SPED. I went to Billy Wilkins house and I remember it smelled like wet dog.

Back to the present.

"Wow, Jack. I mean that's great, buddy," my dad quickly said.

Of course my mom wasn't so easy.

"What friend? Someone we know? Where do they live?" she fired off her questions in about point six seconds.

"Slow down, Sofie. Let him answer one at a time," my dad said.

"It's Xinho Park. My buddy from SPED class," I answered, dipping my fries in some (thankfully normal) ketchup.

"I don't think I know his family. I guess they've never bought paint from us." My mom said the last part as if that made them automatic serial killers.

Wow. The nerve of them not to have freshly painted walls.

"Well that hardly matters, hon," my dad said and then looked at me. "That's just super, JackTrack. It's definitely time you got some friends to chill with outside of school. Friday nights with us old fogies can't be fun."

"We're not old. And we do have fun, don't we, Jack?" my mom said, sounding offended.

"Sure, mom. You aren't too old yet, and Fridays with you are a blast. It's just time I branched out a bit."

No way was I going to tell her about learning to dance. She'd have me at some dance studio learning to waltz or polka before it was even out of my mouth. My mom was like that.

"Well. I guess it's OK. But I need to talk to your friend's mom, and I'll drop you off and pick you up from his house," my mom finally said.

"Why do you have to talk to his mom? And I was going to ride my bike to school tomorrow and ride home with Xin. He rides to school every day."

"I want to talk to his mom because that's what moms do. And as far as riding your bike to school, absolutely not. There are three cross streets between here and Hickory Hills! I'd never let you ride your bike that far!"

I looked to my dad for support, but he was looking down. He snuck a quick glance at me and gave his head a quick shake. I guess he meant to drop it for now and be happy she was at least letting me go.

But I wasn't giving in that easily. My mom was going to have to realize that I wasn't a little kid anymore.

"Mom. I'm not seven. I can ride my bike on 'cross streets,' whatever those are," I argued despite Dad's warning shake.

"A cross street happens to be a very large and very dangerous intersection, Young Man," she said getting worked up.

Uh-oh. "Young Man" meant she was annoyed, big time.

Sigh.

Alright.

Mom won Round One, but Round Two was out there, and I meant to fight it.

After dinner I went to my room and figured I should call Xin so my mom could talk to his. What a hassle!

I mean whose mom calls other moms anyway?

Obviously mine, and I was beginning to see where my genetic Lameness might be coming from.

It hit me then that I hadn't thought to get Xin's number, and when I finally found the phone book, there were about eighty Parks listed. I decided that the easiest thing would be to call Xin's cell instead.

Of course, not having his cell number was a bit of a problem.

I was coming to find out that having friends took preparation, and I wondered what else I didn't know about teenage besties and their habits.

Life was definitely easier when being somebody's friend just meant sharing the shovel in the sandbox.

After racking my brain, I figured that I'd have to call Harper – hers was the only number I had besides my parents – and ask her for Xinho's number, since she'd made a point of getting everyone's info on practically the first day of school.

She definitely had more practice at having friends than me.

Too bad I hadn't learned to text yet. That would be much easier, but I'd been avoiding it because of my dyslexia. With a text, there were no nervous silences or choking on embarrassment or wondering what to say. Just send a couple of quick words and you were home free.

I guess I should put learning to text on my to-do list, too. Though that list was getting kind of long...

1. learn to make friends
2. learn to dance
3. learn to text
4. learn to not be lame

I wasn't about to go ask my dad for a text lesson since I was still mad at my mom for treating me like a baby and I was getting back at her by staying in my room an extra long time.

Hey, wait, that might be irony again. Got to ask McFee.

Back to my present problem...I was determined to have a Friday night away from my parents, and to do that I needed Xin's number. To get Xin's number I needed to call Harper. And to call Harper I needed to climb over the wall of fear I'd built in my mind. Gulp.

I took a deep breath and found her number in my contacts – not hard when there were only three – and hit call. It rang just once before I heard a girl's voice saying "Harper's phone. Is this her Mystery Boyfriend?"

I sat there in shock for a second and didn't know what to say. I heard voices on the other end giggling and whispering.

"I think it's Colin…he's too shy to talk," said the First Girl voice.

"Or maybe Brent, that cute boy in my homeroom," said Another Girl voice.

Oh jeez. They thought I was Colin or someone cute.

"Hellooooo," I heard First Girl say from the other end.

Decide Jack…HangUp or Speak?

My first instinct was to HangUp, but I needed Xinho's number to get out of Friday Night Lameness.

Decide NOW Jack…HangUp or Speak?

I Spoke.

"Um, hi, is Harper there?" I said, and of course my voice squeaked on "there."

Stupid puberty.

"Maybe…it depends on who's calling?" First Girl said.

Sigh. I couldn't lie because Harper would know. I guess I had to tell them who it really was and just be prepared for the reaction.

"It's Jack," I finally said.

"Oh. Harper, it's only Jack," First Girl (who sounded a lot like Britney) said with real disappointment in her voice. "No one good at all," Another Girl added.

I could hear Harper saying, "Britney, stop it!" as she was getting on the line, but the damage was done.

No Good Jack.

Boring Jack.

"Hey Jack. Ignore those lunatics. They're both nuts."

"Um, no problem. Sorry to bother you."

"No bother. What's up?"

"Well, do you happen to have Xin's cell number? I'm going home with him tomorrow after school and I need to get in touch," I said, hoping she'd realize my Friday night plans involved more than my parents and a DVD player.

"Sure. I'll just text it to you. You could've just texted me you know. You didn't have to call and hear these crazy people," she said.

I didn't want to tell her that while I could read a (short) text, I still didn't know how to write one.

"Ahh, well, the texting on this phone's a little weird. I thought it was just easier to call."

"Sure. Whatever is easier I guess. But that phone is really perfect for texting, my mom just got one after she saw yours. Maybe you just need another lesson?"

I heard Britney in the background "He doesn't know how to text???" and Another Girl shrieked with laughter.

Sigh. I guess no one thought about the kid with dyslexia maybe having a hard time texting. I could read short texts with some time, but it was too embarrassing to try to do it in front of people. It was best to just say I didn't know how.

"No worries. I'm sending his number now," Harper said.

"Thanks, bye," I said and I got off the phone as fast as I could.

It wasn't fast enough.

"Ugh, why does HE have your number..." I heard Britney say as I was hanging up.

I was kind of bummed when I called Xinho, but he didn't notice, and we confirmed our hangout plan for tomorrow. I was a little embarrassed to ask him for his home phone number so that my mom could talk to his mom, but he didn't seem to mind. Maybe it was normal for moms to communicate.

There was so much for me to learn about having friends.

I got his address and we hung up. I was getting ready to do my homework when my phone rang (!?!) with a little robot sound. I didn't recognize the number and thought maybe it was Xinho calling me back from somewhere.

"Hello," I said.

"Hi Jack. It's Britney."

Gulp. This couldn't be good. Why would the Queen of Mean even have my number, much less be calling me?

Let's see, maybe she was calling to tell me never to call Harper again? Or to tell me to fall off the earth at the earliest possible moment? I know, maybe she's calling me with advice to give myself a swirly and save Colin the effort.

"Oh. Hi," I answered when I got my brain back to normal.

"Listen. After you and Harper talked, she said that she thought you were super cute. She also said that she hoped you'd ask her to the Fall Festival dance."

I sat there stunned. What was going on?

"Jack? You there?" Britney said.

"Yeah. I'm here."

"So you will definitely ask her to the dance?"

"Um, I don't know. We're pretty much just friends."

"No, I think she wants to be more than friends," Britney said, and I thought I heard faint laughter in the background.

She hung up after that, and while part of me felt excited because Harper (supposedly) liked me, the other part had been put on high alert. Too much Britney was bad for anybody, and I was way over my quota for the week.

CHAPTER SEVENTEEN

The next day at school, Harper acted normal. I didn't get any hints that she "liked" me. I even asked her to share her cookies as a test of her feelings, and she said no.

Not a good sign.

McFee was in a great mood, and even Bernie was smiling some. I guess Fridays will do that to people.

I knew that I only had a little time to ask Harper to the dance since it was next week, but I didn't think I had enough courage to actually go through with it, no matter what Britney had said on the phone.

Of course I trusted Britney about as far as I could throw her, which wasn't far with my toothpick arms. I really should get to the gym.

The day crawled by, and by the end of the afternoon, we were all glad to finally hear Principal Feathers' whiny voice come out of the speaker on the wall.

"Thanks for another great day Hickory Hills. Make sure you get your tickets to the dance. It's happening in just a week from tonight, and you don't want to miss out on any Super Bad Fun."

We all looked at one another and shook our heads. He was bad in a super way.

By the time he got to "all students are dismissed," Xinho and I were walking out the door. The plan was that he'd ride his bike home and I'd meet him there. My mom would just have to drive slow or take a detour to make sure we didn't get there first.

Harper was walking with us towards the front of the school. Here was my chance to talk to her about next Friday. I mean, maybe she really did think I was "super cute" and maybe she really did want me to ask her to the dance.

Yeah, and maybe a Dancing Ferret was about to jump out of her backpack and sing "The Star-Spangled Banner."

I decided to keep my mouth shut for now, and we stood together with all the other car riders waiting on parents.

"No bus today, Jack? Oh, that's right. You're going home with Xin. Cool," she said. "What are you guys going to do?"

No way was I going to tell her the truth about learning to dance, so I just said "You know, hang out. Play some video games. Shoot some hoops." Those sounded like fairly standard guy things to do. Though actually I couldn't shoot a hoop unless it involved a hula.

"Sounds fun," she said as she walked to her mom's sleek car that was pulling up to the curb. "Have a good weekend," she added, closing the car door as her mom waved at me.

"Yeah. You too," I answered and realized a prime dance-asking opportunity had just passed me by.

Dance-Asking Opportunity?? Who was I kidding?

If I even went to the stupid dance, it would be solo. The most I'd hope for would be to stand near Harper, maybe talk a little, and watch her dance with not-lame boys.

Xinho had already taken off on his bike, and I stood in front of the school waiting for my mom. While I waited, I replayed all the conversations from the day that had involved Harper, and I looked for any sign that she "thought I was super cute" like Britney had said. The closest I could get was when Harper had said she liked my new hoodie. Not exactly true-love talk.

The worst part of junk like this was not having anyone to ask about this stuff. I mean, who did guys talk to? Their parents? Nah, I couldn't stand them in my business like that. I could see my mom polling her customers about what I should do.

"Sure, Mrs. Jones, we'll get your red lacquer paint...but first do you think Jack should ask Harper to the dance? I'm taking a little survey..."

Maybe guys tell their friends about girl stuff, and then they help them decide what to do. Since I didn't have any official friends yet, I didn't think that would work for me.

I'd just have to sort it out myself, and I stood on the sidewalk surrounded by screaming kids but feeling pretty alone.

Just then our Über Uncool minivan pulled up, and my mom honked her horn even though she was two feet away. Were all moms so annoying? I knew she meant well, but enough already.

"Hi, Mom," I said getting into the car.

She handed me a pack of crackers and a juice box. "I brought you an afterschool snack."

It was hard to stay annoyed at a mom who did nice stuff for you, so I told her thanks and jammed the whole pack into my mouth. Eating lunch at 11:00 made you super starved by 3:30.

"So how was your day?" she began as we pulled away from the school.

"Fine."

"Any homework for the weekend?"

"Nope," I answered gulping down the juice.

"Are you excited to go visit your friend?"

"Mom. It's not a big deal. He's just a buddy from school," I answered shortly and went back to being annoyed with her. My mom meant well, but she didn't know when to stop with the questions.

"OK, OK. Just asking. Your dad and I actually have our own plans tonight...an early movie and then a nice dinner at Lutece."

Lutece?!? So what happened to rentals and pizza like every other Friday night? I guess with me out of the way they could do better stuff. Now I was definitely annoyed with her.

Mom used her printed directions to get us to Xin's house, and we beat him there. Sitting in his driveway and waiting on him to get home was awkward, but there was no way my mom was leaving me here alone. In her mind, I could be snatched off the street at any given moment.

Finally I saw him pedaling way down the street, and he gradually got closer til he was sitting in the driveway, sweaty and out of breath.

My mom got out of the car (Embarrassment #1 — She Showed Herself!) and went over to say hello.

"Hi there. I'm Mrs. Parker," she said with her crazy paint splattered overalls. (Embarrassment #2 — She Dressed Bad!)

"Um, hi. I'm Xin," he answered, pulling his helmet off of his damp hair.

"I'd like to say hello to your parents, if that's OK." (Embarrassment #3 — She Is Overprotective!) She already got to see the house and meet my friend. What's her deal!?

"Well, actually my folks don't get home from work til around five, so it'll be awhile."

"That's OK. I can wait." (Embarrassment #4 — She Won't Leave!) Whose mom sits in a driveway and waits to meet parents?!

"Mom! You don't have to wait! We're just going to be hanging out here playing video games. I'm by myself at our house until you get home from work...what's the difference?"

"Well, you boys might get into some mischief," she said. (Embarrassment #5 — She Said Mischief!)

Just then her phone started ringing with my dad's ringtone that sounded like a dying whale and she answered it.

"Hello," she said.

She was quiet and listened to my dad for a few seconds, staring at me while he talked to her.

"OK. Give me a minute," she finished. "Bye."

She turned off her phone and put her hands on her hips. "So your dad has a crisis at the store, and I have to go help him. All the paint rollers fell off their display and it's a huge mess and a safety hazard."

"Sweet," I said with a small smile. "I mean darn."

"You boys behave yourselves til Xinho's parents get home," she said as she got back into the minivan.

She stuck her head out of the window as she was backing out of the driveway and said, "Call me if you need me. Don't be bad. Don't use the stove."

"We won't," Xin and I both said in unison and then started cracking up.

"Bye, Jack, I love you," she shouted as she was pulling away (Embarrassment #6 — She Shouted About Love!) Wow six in two minutes had to be some kind of record for her. Luckily there was no one on the street, and since Xinho already knew how crazy she was, the damage was done.

"Wow," Xin finally said as she pulled out of sight. "She makes my Asian Tiger Mom look like a kitten. Sorry, dude."

"I know, right? She means well, but she's like a sweater that's too tight or something. She just makes me feel like I'm suffocating."

"Moms are weird. Come on, let's get something to eat. I'm starving."

As we walked into the house, I noticed the school bus stopping a few blocks away.

"Pretty cool that you can beat the bus home."

"Yeah, I wouldn't ride that bus for anything. It's worth the cold or rain or bugs in my mouth to stay away from that torture chamber"

"Is that Leo getting off the bus?"

"Yeah, he lives behind my house, but he gets off at the first stop and walks the rest of the way. It cuts down on his torture time, too," Xin said.

I tried to picture what a bus ride must be like for the Leos of the world, and I couldn't imagine. Somehow I was lucky enough to get pretty girls and harmless boys on my bus, but I knew that Xin had been bullied on his bus, so there must be rough stuff going on.

"Does Leo ever ride his bike to school?"

"I don't think he has a bike...honestly, I don't think he has much at all," Xin said with a sad look on his face. "I'm not talking about the dude behind his back, you know Leo's my man," Xin continued. "But I hear some ugly things from his house. You'll see. Fridays are the worst day for him..."

I was seriously confused about what Xinho was talking about as we walked through his kitchen to the back deck. The deck was two stories, so you could see a pretty good way from up there.

"That's where Leo lives," he said as he pointed to a shabby looking house through the trees.

I saw a faded green house with lots of junk in the yard and weeds growing everywhere. As we stared, we saw Leo come through the back yard fence and let himself into the house through the back door. He wasn't inside a minute before I heard voices yelling.

"That's his dad. He's gotten pretty crazy over the last year. Sometimes on Fridays, Mr. Delaney gets drunk and comes out on their back porch screaming at Leo or the neighbors. It's pretty rough."

"Jeez. Does he hurt Leo? I mean, hit him?"

"I don't think so, but what he says is messed up. Poor kid. Tells Leo how worthless he is and how he'll never be a man. I've tried to get Leo to come over here sometimes, but he likes to keep an eye on his little sisters. The dad's mental for sure."

Even from Xin's deck, we could hear a loud voice yelling over at Leo's house and a door slamming.

I thought about my own Friday nights and how easy and fun they were. I wouldn't ever call them boring again. I thought too about how I really had never reached out to Leo because I didn't want Colin or his crowd to see me as Leo's friend and decide I'd be a better target.

What a lousy person I must be...

Xinho saw the look on my face and patted my back. "I know, dude. It sucks. I wish I could help him, but I don't know how. My parents tried talking to the dad once, and he ran them off the porch."

"I wonder if McFee could help."

"Leo has asked me not to ever say anything at school about his home junk. He just tries to get through."

"No wonder he sleeps under the bed..."

"I know, right? OK...sorry for the bummer. Let's eat a snack and see if we can teach you to dance...hopefully you have some rhythm," he said and headed back into the kitchen.

"Rhythm? I doubt it!" I said as I followed along and tried to shake the mental image of Leo crouched under his bed from my brain.

The rhythm took a minute to find, but it was in there somewhere. Xin actually taught me a few good moves that I put together with some things of my own that I honestly never knew that I could do. All in all, I got through our dance lesson without too many problems.

We decided to take a break just before seven, and my phone started ringing. I hoped it wasn't my mom saying that she was coming early to get me, but when I looked at the screen I saw that it was Harper calling.

Harper calling me? On a Friday night? The world must be ending.

"Hello," I said after I gave Xin a what-the-heck? look and showed him her name on my screen.

"Hi, Jack. It's Harper," she said.

"Um, hi, Harper. So what's up?"

"Not much," I heard her say and then heard voices in the background. "What are you guys up to?"

I gave Xin a look of confusion and shook my head. "Not much here either, just playing video games and chilling."

I heard Britney say, "Did he ask you?" in the background.

"Britney stop it," Harper answered though she must have had her hand on the phone or something because her voice was muffled.

"Well, Britney told me to call you because she said you had something to ask me, but if you don't, you know, have anything to ask, then I guess I'll be going."

Britney screamed "You should ask him!" and loud laughter erupted from somewhere.

Now my stomach felt sick, and I knew that I was the butt of their joke. Britney must have told Harper that I wanted to ask her to the dance, and that was why she was calling. I couldn't believe Harper was going along with this mean prank, but I guess when you wanted to be popular you'd do just about anything.

Even if it meant hurting a friend.

I could still hear the loud shrieks of laughter in the background when Harper got back on the phone. "I gotta go, Jack. Bye," she said and was gone like that.

"Um, bye," I said to a dead phone.

"That was weird," Xin said as he pressed play on the video game remote. "Girls are sure hard to figure out...I didn't even know Harper liked you."

"Britney just told her to call me as a joke to see if I was dumb enough to say something embarrassing. It gave them something to do for a minute and now they'll move on to harassing someone else."

"I wouldn't have thought Harper had the Mean Girl Gene, but I guess Britney can be pretty convincing," Xin said, and he went back to shooting mutant aliens.

I still felt a little sick to my stomach and I knew my face was red from embarrassment, so I walked outside onto Xin's deck to get some air.

When I was outside on the deck, I looked over to Leo's place and saw him sitting in a lawn chair in the corner of his yard. He was reading a book, even though it was getting dark and it had to be hard to see. I wanted to talk to him, but I didn't want to raise my voice and get his crazy dad's attention.

I walked carefully down the steps of Xin's deck and went back to the corner of his yard that was closest to Leo's place.

Peeking through the fence, I semi-whispered "Hey, Leo. Hi," and his head came up in a flash. He looked immediately up at his house and made sure no one had heard or was out on the porch.

"Hi, Jack. You visiting Xin or something?" he said.

"Yeah, he's trying to teach me to dance," I answered and told him the truth without a second thought. No way was I going to try and lie to Leo. "I'm hoping Harper will maybe give me at least one pity dance at the Fall Festival next week."

"I'm sure she will. She likes you," he answered.

"No. I don't think I fall in the like category for her, but it's fine. So, um, Xin told me that things are pretty rough around here. I'm sorry, Leo."

"Thanks, Jack. My dad's always been a little hard on us, but since he lost his job he's ten times worse. My mom's working three jobs just to keep things going, so I don't want to bug her about it."

"Man. That sucks. I had no idea," I said.

"Well, it is what it is," Leo said with a small smile. "That's Bernie talk for sure. I figure it won't always be this way, right?" He waited for me to respond, but I didn't have anything to say.

"Anyway, I try to keep the same attitude about all the junk with bullies at school," he went on. "I don't want to tell McFee or anyone about Colin because the school might call here to tell my dad...that would definitely make it worse for me at home...so I just try to ignore them and hope it gets better."

"But maybe someone could help if you told," I said, not even sure if I was talking about getting Leo help for the bullies at school or the bully at home.

"No, it's easier to just keep quiet. Plus with Bernie on my side, Colin has definitely been keeping his distance," Leo said.

"That's good," I said.

"Being at school also gets me away from home, and I get to see good friends like you," he said with a shy smile.

I remembered how many times I'd turned the other way when Leo was getting harassed at school, and yet he still called me a friend. I didn't deserve that title.

"Thanks, Leo. I consider you my friend, too, so it worries me that your dad's so crazy. Isn't there anything someone can do?" I asked.

"Not really. He's my dad. I mean if he wasn't screaming at me, he'd be screaming at my little sisters, and that'd be worse," he said, quickly looking at the house as we heard a crashing noise.

"So you just deal with it?"

"Yup. I deal cause if I didn't deal, then I'm scared that they would put us in foster care like Bernie," he said as he listened for more noises from the house. "Hey, it's getting dark, so I better go inside before he starts yelling and the neighbors hear."

"Bye, Leo. And don't worry. I won't say anything to Ms. McFee."

"Thanks, Jack. See you Monday," Leo finished as he turned to walk up to the sad-looking house.

All thoughts of Harper and Britney and her lame group of friends (Hey, maybe I wasn't the lame one after all!?!) went out of my head as I watched Leo trudge up to his house in the fading light. His blond curls were about all I could see as he went into the dark house.

That poor kid.

I was whining about my overprotective mom, while his mom was never home when his dad went crazy and yelled at Leo. It wasn't right, but what could be done?

Just then I heard Xin from up on his deck. "Hey, Jack...your mom's here."

Of course she came thirty minutes early! I ran up the steps to grab my stuff and say goodbye to Xin.

"Thanks for giving me moves like Jagger," I said as I walked to the front door.

"No problem, my brother. Now you just gotta use the moves next week at the dance," Xin answered as he held the door open for me.

"Sure. I'll have a great time dancing with myself!" I laughed. "See you Monday."

I climbed into my lame minivan with my definitely uncool mom and felt grateful for what I had.

"Sorry to be early, but we finished dinner and I didn't want to be out too late driving in the dark," my mom said. I could tell she was worried I'd be mad.

"No problem, Mom. Thanks for coming to get me," I said and she looked surprised. "No. I really mean it. Thanks."

As we drove home, the visions of Leo reading outside in the near dark and walking into the gloomy house wouldn't leave me. I wondered what his weekend would be like.

How bad must life be in his sad little house that he preferred the bullies at school to his dad at home?

CHAPTER EIGHTEEN

The remainder of the weekend went by normally (code-word for dull) with chores and helping at the store on Saturday and then football watching with my dad on Sunday.

Over the weekend, I locked the bathroom door a couple of times and put on my headset to practice dancing, but my mom kept banging on the door and asking what all the thumping was about. I was trying to stay grateful for not having crazy parents like Leo's, but she made it pretty tough sometimes.

Thoughts of Leo didn't leave my mind too often, and I struggled to figure out what the heck to do. Xin and his parents had tried to help, but maybe I could try again. I spent all weekend planning out who was the best person to talk to.

Telling my parents was out. My mom would have a SWAT team surrounding Leo's house in five minutes, and it would be all over the news. "Local Dad Yells at Son. Video at Eleven."

Walking into school from the bus on Monday morning, I considered talking to the counselor at school, Mrs. Schmidt, but she never really listened to kids. She just gave them a lecture about the dangers of inhalants and sent them on their way with a peppermint.

Next was McFee, but Leo had specifically told Xin and me not to tell her and I'd said that I wouldn't. I didn't want to break his trust like that.

Who did that leave? Bernie? No, she had enough to worry about with not knowing where the heck she'd be living in a month. Bryce? He'd just stare at me or maybe go pound on Leo's dad for a bit. While that would be awesome, it really wouldn't help in the long run.

Before Friday night's phone call, I'd have gone straight to Harper and asked her what we should do. I mean, when she first joined SGS, she seemed like she cared about people or something.

But then she called me just to embarrass me, and that definitely wasn't cool.

Though she'd said her mom liked a cause, and what better cause than a kid whose dad was semi-crazy? Still, could I trust her not to blab everything about Leo's home life to Britney and her clique?

It was so hard to know what to do for Leo, and my mind wasn't on school at all that morning. I didn't even hear Feathers or his announcements, and McFee's voice was like a faraway buzz in my ears.

Seeing Harper in class made the morning even worse, and I'd spent the whole math lesson deliberately not making eye contact, which is hard in such a small space.

I mean, you can only look at the wall for so long.

McFee had asked if I was OK because I wasn't contributing any answers to her Geometry review game, and I'm usually her go-to math genius. I told her that I'd had a long weekend of doing super fun and important stuff, but that I'd try to rally after lunch.

After wracking my brain when I was supposed to be learning math, I finally decided that Harper was the best (only) choice to talk to about Leo because her mom didn't seem crazy like mine and could maybe even help. How I was going to tell her about Leo I didn't know, since Harper hadn't even looked at me all morning (though how would I know that if I hadn't looked at her??) and I figured she didn't want anything else to do with me after the "phone call."

By the middle of the morning it was break time, and we all walked out of class and headed towards the bathrooms or water fountains. While I dreaded talking to someone who enjoyed making fun of me, I remembered that this was for Leo and knew it was something I had to do.

"Hi, Harper. Did you have a good weekend?" I said, trying to sound normal as we all headed down the hall.

She jumped a little with surprise when I spoke to her, but we kept walking towards the water fountain.

"Um. Hi, Jack," she said and then stopped in the hall. "I definitely didn't have a good weekend."

"Sorry about that. Did you break a nail or did you run out of boys to call and embarrass?"

Argghhhh!!! I'd promised myself that I was only going to talk about Leo and I wasn't going to bring up the humiliating phone call, but my stupid mouth didn't get the message!

Harper's face turned a little red, and she looked down at the floor quickly. "I'm really sorry for that, Jack. I swear it wasn't my idea."

"Maybe not, but you went along with it," I said as I bent over to get some water.

"I know. I've felt terrible all weekend. It's just so hard. I want to be your friend, but I want to be Britney's friend too, and she makes it tough," Harper said.

"Whatever. You do what you need to do. I know that being popular has been tops on your list since you got here," I said.

"Jack, listen..." Harper began.

I interrupted her, "But I do need your help with something more important than Britney and her stupid games."

That got her attention.

"Leo has some problems at home...I can't tell you about it right now...but I wonder if your mom could maybe help us."

"My mom? Sure, I mean I can pretty much tell her anything and she doesn't freak out too badly," she said as we stood in the center of the hallway.

"Great. Can you call me this afternoon after school?"

"Well, why don't you just come home with me? I mean, my mom picks me up anyway, and we can talk in the car."

What was happening? I'd gone from being mad at Harper to having the opportunity to ride in her car, go to her house, and maybe (gulp) see her room??

This couldn't be real!

"Um. Well. I need to ask my folks," I said.

"Look. Just take your phone into the boys' room and text your dad. He's the nice one, right?"

I couldn't believe she already knew which parent was the easiest mark.

"Yeah. For sure. I'll do that," I answered, still in a daze. As I walked into the boys' bathroom, I wondered if I'd always be so easily swayed by a girl.

As long as they looked like Harper, that would be a yes.

Now the challenge of texting began. No way was I going outside to ask Harper for help. I took out my phone and stared at it, hoping I'd think of something.

Just then a random seventh grader who rode my bus walked in and looked at me staring helplessly at my phone.

"Need some help? My older sister has that phone, and I hack into all the time to read her creepy texts to her boyfriend."

"Um. Thanks. That'd be great," I answered. "I just want to text my dad and tell him that I'm riding home with Harper today after school."

The kid looked at me with new respect. "Blonde Harper with the great smile?"

I nodded.

"Well done, my man," he said as he gave me a fist bump and took my phone.

Thirty seconds later, my dad texted back.

It took me a minute to read his text, but my dad knows to use short words if he's writing me a note or anything. He'd written, "Get It JackAttack! I'll handle Mom. Txt me l8r ;)"

The winky face made me smile, but then I realized that LameJack was going to a (gulp) girl's house, and I'd never been so scared in my life.

The rest of the afternoon went by as slowly as my granddad drives, and when it finally came time for announcements, my stomach was in knots.

As Feathers rattled on, I tried to calm down by re-minding myself that I was just going to hang out with Harper. We weren't getting married or going to kiss or anything.

Agghhhh!! Why had I thought of kissing her? What if she sensed that I had thought about kissing her and was disgusted by my presence?

The whole idea of going home with Harper suddenly seemed nuts, and I was a split second away from sprint-ing to the buses and forgetting about it all.

But then I caught a glimpse of Leo as he waited to be dismissed. The dark circles under his eyes and his bony arms and legs sticking out of his faded T-shirt and too short jeans made me stop thinking about myself and kissing anyone.

I remembered the entire reason for going home with Harper, and I calmed down instantly.

Helping other people made you forget about your own problems, and I realized that was a good thing. I knew for sure that if this was a way to help Leo, then I had to suck it up and get over my fear of spending time alone with Harper.

Though maybe I'd still think about kissing her.

And getting my braces caught in her lips.

Scratch that idea.

Principal Feathers finally let us go, and Harper, Xin, and I walked to the front of the school. Xin looked curiously at me since I came with them instead of heading to the buses.

"Orthodontist appointment, Jackster?" he asked.

"No," Harper jumped in immediately. "Jack's coming home with me."

Xin's head jerked up and he gave me a huge grin. "Awesome, my brother," he said with a wiggle of his eyebrows. "High Five!" he added, sticking his hand up for a slap.

"Oh, don't be silly. I mean, Jack's great, but it's nothing like that," Harper said with a smile.

Thoughts of kissing faded like a poof of smoke in my feverish brain.

"Yeah, nothing like that," I echoed.

"Jack wants my mom to help with something about Leo."

Xin looked at me with surprise. "Cool. That kid needs some help. My folks and I tried, but we didn't get anywhere...he definitely deserves a break."

We'd made it to the front doors, and now Harper looked concerned.

"Wow. I don't know what's going on with Leo, but you guys are freaking me out a little bit," Harper said as she pushed through the door along with all the other middle schoolers eager for their freedom.

"Jack'll tell you. It's pretty rough. Catch you guys later," Xin said as he headed to unlock his bike.

Harper and I stood awkwardly on the sidewalk and waited for her mom. I thought about telling her Leo's story, but I knew I'd have to tell her mom, too, so I waited.

Just then Colin and Britney walked out of the school, followed by a pack of laughing kids. They both looked at Harper and me and stopped short.

"Hi, Harper, what's up?" Britney said with her hands on her hips as she looked at me with curiosity.

"Hey, Harper...long time no see," added Colin.

Out of habit I stepped back so that Colin wouldn't notice me. I didn't want to be a target on his bully radar too.

"Hey, people. Not much here...just waiting for my mom," Harper said.

"We're walking to McDonald's, Harper. Wanna go?" Colin asked.

"No, thanks. Jack's coming home with me to work on a project."

"I didn't think you SPED heads had to do homework," Colin said.

"Don't be stupid. Of course we do homework," Harper said, getting angry.

"Hey, no offense, I was just saying," Colin began.

"Shut up, Colin," Britney cut him off. "If Harper wants to hang with Dweeber here and do 'homework,' that's her business. Just know that you can't have it both ways, Princess."

The two girls stared at each other. Neither one looked away.

"What do you mean?" Colin asked.

"Oh, nothing. Come on, let's go. We'll let these two have their little after school special."

And like that, they were off, and all the kids waiting on the sidewalk moved aside to let them pass. It was like the parting of the seas for the "popular kids." Or maybe the kids moved out of the way to avoid being noticed like me.

I felt badly for not saying a word to defend myself or Harper, but I hadn't.

"What was that about? What did she mean by having it both ways?" I asked Harper, though I was pretty sure I knew the answer.

"Oh nothing. She's just silly sometimes. Hey, there's my mom."

Sure enough, the sleek Mercedes pulled up, and I could see Harper's mom smiling in the driver's seat.

"Hi, honey. Hi, Jack." Mrs. Finley said as we climbed in.

"Hi, Mom."

"Hello, Mrs. Finley. Thanks for letting me come home with Harper," I said.

"Of course, Jack. Harper texted me that you need my help with something, but she didn't know what," Mrs. Finley said as she pulled out of the parking lot.

I climbed into the back seat of the car and began, "Well, it's kind of a long story, but here goes…"

CHAPTER NINETEEN

I spent a couple of hours at Harper's (amazing) house, and I definitely felt better after I told an adult what was going on at Leo's place. Mrs. Finley said she'd give it some serious thought and talk to her husband to see what they could do to help.

I didn't get to see Harper's room or kiss her.

Shocking.

My dad had apparently smoothed things with my mom about my going home with Harper, and they both picked me up at 6:30. As I climbed into the minivan, I waited for my mom to start with twenty questions about Harper, her family, her house, and what kind of milk was in their fridge (soy or almond?).

"That phone is working for you already, JackSmack. Going home with a girl is big stuff," my dad said as we pulled out of Harper's neighborhood.

"Very funny, Dad, but it's nothing like that. We were just doing some school junk," I said as I settled into the back seat, prepared for my mom's quiz over Harper and the paint colors in her house.

"Whatever you say, buddy. How about dinner out tonight?"

Eating out during the week was unusual for us, but I was all for it.

Anything to avoid my mom's Monday Night Salmon-loaf (healthier than meatloaf and a million times more disgusting).

"Sure, Dad. Sounds great. Are we celebrating something?" I asked.

"No, not really. Just wanted to shake things up a bit, you know. Change our routine."

"Or did Mom burn the Salmonloaf again?" I asked.

"Jack! I never burn dinner!" my mom said, and both my dad and I looked at each other and laughed.

When we pulled up at the Italian Oven, there wasn't a big crowd, so they sat us down quickly at a booth in the corner of the restaurant. My dad asked about my day, and I lied and said I'd had a pretty good day. No way I was going to tell him and Mom about Leo and his crazy dad. I could still see visions of the SWAT team if my mom got wind of Leo's dad and the way he treated Leo.

I was studying the menu and trying to decide between chicken parmesan or spaghetti and meatballs when my mom said out of nowhere, "We need to get you a suit to wear to the dance on Friday."

Dance? Friday?

With all the Leo craziness and going home with Harper, I'd totally forgotten the dance was this week!

"A suit? No, mom...I can wear jeans. It's just a school dance," I said as I tore into the breadbasket.

"Oh. Well what about a new shirt? A nice Oxford with a button-down collar?"

Since when did my mom become my fashion advisor?

"No thanks, Mom. I'll just wear something I have. It's really not that big a deal."

"Not a big deal? It's your first school dance! Next thing you know you'll be going to prom and then you'll graduate," she said, looking sad.

"Mom. Get a grip. It's just a dance, and I'm just in eighth grade. I'll be around a while yet."

My dad laughed and told my mom to cool it as we ordered our dinner. He definitely must have told her not to give me the third degree about Harper because we made it all the way to dessert before she asked me how my "afternoon went."

My dad shot her a look, but I said, "It's OK, Dad. I'm sure she's dying from curiosity."

I was talking to my parents and making up stuff about the nonexistent science project that Harper and I'd been working on when I saw a familiar figure walking into the restaurant.

I started to wave to Bernie and about choked on my cheesecake when McFee came in right behind her!

McFee saw us immediately, and she and Bernie came right over to our table. I'd spent the last two years in Ms. McFee's class, so my parents knew her pretty well.

"Hi, Ms. McFee," my dad said as he stood up to say hello.

"How great to see you! What a surprise!" my mom said as she jumped up and gave McFee a hug.

"Yeah. Great to see you, too. Bernie and I are just grabbing a bite to eat," McFee said.

"Bernie, this is Mr. and Mrs. Parker, Jack's parents," she continued.

"Mom, Dad, I've told you about Bernie. She's the one who always tells us when we smell," I added.

"Good! Someone needs to tell you! Nice to meet you, Bernie," my mom said and extended her hand for Bernie to shake it.

"Um. Nice to meet y'all too. And all I smell in here is delicious!" Bernie said.

We laughed and my mom went on. "We just picked up Jack from Harper's house. They were working on a science project."

"Science project?" McFee asked, and I saw Bernie step on her toe.

"Yeah, McFee, you know the one that you assigned? The real sciencey one about science?" Bernie went on trying to save my butt.

"Oh. Sure. Now I remember. That science project. Glad you two are getting a head start on that one..." McFee went along with the bogus science project story quite nicely. I guess because she knew my mom would freak if she found out that I went to a girl's house for anything other than schoolwork.

I'd have to thank them both tomorrow.

"Bernie, are you going to the dance on Friday?" my NosyMom asked.

"Yeah. Probably. I told Leo I'd go, and I can't leave him without a dance partner."

"You think he'll be able to go, Ms. McFee? His dad seems kind of, well, strict," I said not wanting to let on how bad Mr. Delaney really was.

"I hope so. I sent an email to everyone's parents with information about the times of the dance and everything. So hopefully Leo's dad will let him come. He's a little hard to predict though," Ms. McFee said.

A little hard to predict? That seemed like saying dynamite could be a little dangerous, but I didn't want to take that topic any further right now. I wracked my brain for something else to talk about.

Then I remembered.

"So Ms. McFee, when are you going to talk to the high school about getting us out of small group for next year?"

McFee's smile disappeared. "I don't know, Jack. Honestly, I don't. Principal Feathers is pretty against us having SPED kids in regular classes in middle school, and without our having the program at Hickory Hills, the high school won't offer it either."

"That's stupid. Why should Feathers care about us being in the regular classes? You could still work with the SPED kids, but just in a normal class instead of our isolation ward," I said.

"Yeah, that's what Goldilocks said they did in her old school. Kids get the extra help they need without being locked away by themselves all year," Bernie added.

"Stop it. Both of you," my mom began. "It's not Ms. McFee's fault or her decision to keep you in small group. The school makes that call."

"Well, maybe they need to change the call," my dad said quietly, and my mom stared at him in surprise. "I mean it, Sofie. Who says it's better for Jack and kids like him to be separate from all the other kids all day? No offense to you, Ms. McFee. You're amazing. But I have to wonder if this is in the kids' long-term best interest. I sent a letter to the Board of Education with my concerns, so we'll see what they say."

Wait...what?

Since that day we argued about it, my dad had never said another word about my SPED placement and what was going to happen to me in high school. I thought he'd forgotten about it. Now I find out he's ready to take on the Board of Education?

Go Dad!

"Wow. Well keep me posted," McFee said. "It's hard sometimes for teachers to rock the boat and question things, but for parents it's a little easier. I only want what's best for my kids. You know that."

"Speaking of what's best. What should I order, Jack?" Bernie said. "I'm pretty hungry!"

I gave her my recommendations and she smiled at me.

"Nice job with that science project stuff, Mr. Jack. Keep up the good work," she said as McFee motioned to the hostess that they were ready to be seated.

Bernie had known from day one that I had a crush on Harper, so I wasn't surprised that she suspected something. Maybe I'd tell her the truth about the reason I went to Harper's. She was Leo's friend and would want to know what he was dealing with.

The two of them walked off after goodbyes, and we finished our cheesecake and cannolis. My mom watched them walk away and said, "That lady's a saint. Teaching you kids all day and then taking Bernie out to dinner at night. She needs a medal or something."

"Yeah. She's pretty cool. Though she's never taken me out to eat," I said as I stuffed the last bite of cheese-cake in my mouth. "The school cafeteria doesn't count!"

My dad paid the check, and I realized that I definitely liked going out to dinner on a Monday. It started the week off much better then Mom's Monday Salmonloaf. I'd have to think of a reason to do it again next Monday, but without insulting my mom's cooking.

That could be tricky.

The other thing besides chicken parmesan that had me feeling good was the fact that my dad had my back

146

on the whole SPED thing. I thought he'd forgotten all about getting me out of SGS, but he'd gone straight to the school board. Parents could sure surprise you sometimes.

This week was definitely starting right, but with the dance on Friday, who knew how it would end.

CHAPTER TWENTY

The next day at school began with Principal Feathers making his morning announcements as usual. He said what was for lunch and that Conference Week was approaching and that dance tickets would be on sale Wednesday and Thursday during lunch in the cafeteria.

Since I'd definitely decided to go to the dance, I wrote myself a reminder on the palm of my hand to bring money the next day for my ticket. Though I had to admit that even after Xin's lessons I didn't know how much actual *dancing* I'd do at the dance.

Flapping my arms around in a room full of teens and semi-teens sounded like a great way to get on YouTube.

Everyone had filed in from the buses or their moms' car. Bernie was in a great mood, and she started teasing me immediately.

"Hey, Jack...how's that science project going?" she asked.

Xin looked panicked. "What science project? When is it due?"

"It's a science project just for Harper and Jack...they gotta see if they have 'chemistry!'" And she burst out laughing at her own lame joke.

"Ahhhh. I get it," Xin said when he remembered that he'd seen us going home together yesterday.

Harper laughed. "Shut up you two. Jack and I are just friends."

Oh yeah, Just Friends.

Sigh.

Well "just friends" was better than "loser she called on the phone to make fun of," so I supposed I'd take it.

During this whole conversation, Skeever and Leo had been talking quietly. Skeever looked up.

"Attention, people. I have an important announcement when Feathers is done with his lame announcements," Skeever said.

Just then we heard Feathers signing off with his usual "make it a great day or not, the choice is yours." When would he come up with another slogan?

We all looked at Skeever and waited for his announcement.

"Leo here has just informed me that he will be attending Friday's dance, so it looks like we'll all be there to partay like rock stars."

"Yeah, my dad said he didn't care as long as he didn't have to give me any money," Leo added.

"Great, dude. My folks can give you a ride," Xin said.

"Perfect, and I'll buy an extra ticket to give you. It'll be fun," Harper said, which reminded me that she could be a decent person when she wasn't trying to fit in with the Britney Bunch.

Though I had to wonder how she'd balance her SPED Friends and her Snotty Friends at the dance. I pictured her going back and forth between the Cools and the NotCools...that would be a rough one.

"We gonna bring it SPED-style," Bernie added, doing a booty shake. "Hickory Hills Middle won't know what hit it, y'all."

I looked at Bryce and said, "What about you, Bryce, are you coming?"

Bryce nodded once and gave me a thumbs up. Those two things combined were like he'd stood up and made a speech to the class.

"Sweet," Xin said. "The SPED crew will be in the house. Now, you know that I can take any of you in a dance contest, right? Cause I'm the only one in here with moves?"

"But I thought you gave Jack a dance lesson so he could dance with Harper?" Leo said innocently.

"Um..well..." I began awkwardly as all six faces turned to look at me. Leo looked guilty as he realized he'd put his foot in it, Bernie nodded like she'd known all along, Skeever and Xin both looked embarrassed for me, Bryce gave another thumbs up, and Harper was smiling.

Smiling?

"Oh wow, what a nerd" smiling or "Oh goody, we can dance" smiling?

Luckily McFee saved me from falling further into a pit of shame by telling us it was time to get to work.

I never thought I'd say it, but thank goodness for grammar!

CHAPTER TWENTY-ONE

The next day Harper sat by me during lunch in the classroom and said that she needed to talk to me about something private.

Xin and Skeever were playing a video game on Skeev's iTouch, Bryce was reading while he went through his stack of four sandwiches, and Bernie and Leo were sitting by McFee's desk talking to her while they all ate. No one was paying Harper and me any attention.

"So my mom talked to my stepdad," she began as she moved her desk closer to me. Our knees were really close together, and that made me nervous—but in a good way.

"Um, yeah?" I said trying to focus on her words and not our knees.

"Yeah. You know, about Leo and his dad and all."

"Oh!" Light Bulb Moment. How did I get so preoccupied with our stupid knees that I forgot my friend's dad was a jerk and that Harper's mom was looking for a way to help?

And Skeever's the one with ADD!? Focus, Jack!

"Yeah. So anyway, my dad may have a job at his company for Mr. Delaney. It's not a great job or anything, but it's a job. The best part is that he'd be working nights! He won't have a chance to yell so much if Leo's at school all day and then he's working nights!"

"That's amazing. Your parents are awesome."

"I told you my mom loves a cause," Harper said, taking a tiny bite of her apple.

"I hope it happens. Leo deserves a break," I said, eating what the cafeteria had advertised as a hamburger but more closely resembled a hockey puck.

Just then Colin and Britney came to the door and saw Harper and me talking.

"How cute. A private lunch for just the two of you," Britney sneered and both Harper and I jumped in our chairs.

McFee looked at the door in annoyance. "Can I help you?"

"Yes, ma'am," Colin took over. "Principal Feathers sent us to tell all the classes they get to nominate someone to represent their homeroom in the Fall Festival FunRun. It's like a competitive obstacle course."

We all looked at each other with suspicion. Since when did Feathers include us in anything? Maybe the letter from my dad to the school board was doing a little good.

"Not sure why he's including you SPED...I mean 'special' kids, but it really doesn't matter who you send to get slaughtered by yours truly."

Colin looked around at our pitifully small class, "It can be a boy or girl...though you don't have much to choose from, do you?"

"Colin. That's enough," McFee said as she stood up and walked towards the door where Colin and Britney stood. "I don't care how much money your dad gives the school. I've about had it with you. You've delivered your message, and now you can leave."

Bernie slid up to the door just in front of Ms. McFee and stared hard at Colin. "How is the Bully Busters going by the way...are you making Hickory Hills safe for *all* its students?"

If Bernie was trying to embarrass Colin by mentioning Bully Busters while he was busy bullying kids, it wouldn't work. That boy didn't have a sympathetic bone in his creepy body. I knew Colin had been keeping his distance from Leo because somehow Bernie had frightened him off, but I was sure he was making up for it by torturing poor sixth graders in his spare time.

"Absolutely. In fact, my dad had some signs printed with my picture and the Bully Busters logo. They'll be going up tomorrow," he said.

I looked forward to drawing mustaches and horns and monster zits on as many posters as I could, but I still just sat and didn't say a word. As awful as it sounded, I didn't want to draw attention to myself and get on Colin's bad side. Being noticed by Britney was enough.

Bernie, though, had no problem drawing Colin's attention. She stood in the doorway with her arms crossed over her skinny chest and just stared at him.

"Can't wait to see those pictures. Hopefully they Photoshopped that big zit off of your nose," Bernie said.

Colin's hand went to his nose where there really was a monster zit. Maybe I'd only have to draw mustaches and horns I thought and laughed aloud.

"What are you laughing at, Parker? At least I don't have a brace face..."

Uh-oh. Colin had noticed me. I hunched over my lunch and felt my face burn with shame, but I still kept quiet.

McFee had definitely heard enough as she closed the door in their faces and turned to look at us all. I thought she'd say what a loser Colin was, but she didn't even mention his name.

"Fall Festival FunRun participant? Hmmm. We'll need to vote pretty quickly. The dance is in two days..."

Two Days!

The week was flying by at warp speed. All of a sudden it was Wednesday, and the dance was Friday. I didn't know why I was so nervous...I wasn't taking Harper to the dance or anything, and I didn't even have to try and talk to her if I didn't want to.

But I did want to talk to her, and that was the problem. I wanted to try to actually *dance* with her if I got the chance, and that's what was making me nervous.

Wait.

Something very important and very obvious oc-curred to me as McFee was telling us to vote on who we wanted to represent our class in the FunRun.

As I was writing "Duh, Bryce, of course!!!!" on a tiny piece of paper, I was also thinking about the dance and the actual *dancing* part.

I hadn't worked out whether I was going to dance with Harper to a slow song or fast one. Xin and I'd only worked on fast songs with a beat, but I wondered if Harper would want to dance a (gulp) slow song with me? Slow songs meant you actually put your hands on your partner and (gulp again) touched!

The whole slow dancing thing was a mystery since I'd never been to a school dance before, but I'd seen people slow dancing on TV or maybe a Disney movie. What I remembered happening was that the boy asked the girl to dance and then the couple stared into each other's eyes on the dance floor.

After that the world stopped turning, and they had a slow-mo kiss.

Pretty sure that the kiss part wouldn't be happening to me on Friday night since Harper and I were "just friends," but I still wanted to (somehow) be ready for a slow song and I didn't think Xin could help me with that!

CHAPTER TWENTY-TWO

That night at dinner I told my folks about the FunRun and the fact that our SGS class had all voted for Bryce to represent us.

McFee had explained that the FunRun was like an obstacle course that the chosen students did before the actual dance started. The course went around the whole gym, and the students from each homeroom raced against each other.

Wouldn't it be a trip if the SPED-ers won something like that! It'd be so incredibly awesome to have our class be the best at *something*.

While I was clearing the table after dinner, I thought again about my slow dance problem. This was one of those times when I would've liked an older sister or cousin to ask about the ins and outs of dancing with a girl.

It sucked that the only people I had to ask were my parents.

But honestly, I thought as I scrubbed leftover tofu mash (why me?) from a plate and put it in the dishwasher, what was worse?

Current Embarrassment in front of my folks or Future Embarrassment at the dance?

I saw myself finally getting the nerve to ask Harper to dance on a slow song and then tromping her foot or breaking her shoe or something.

With that image in my brain, Fear of Future Embarrassment won out, and I walked into the den where both of my parents were on the couch watching some lame PBS show on the Civil War.

"So, um, I have a little question for you people," I began.

"Shoot, JackAlack," my dad said.

"Is something wrong?" my mom added. She was definitely a glass half empty kinda lady. She always looked for the bad instead of the good.

"No, Mom. Nothing's wrong. Nothing too bad anyway," I went on…feeling super awkward about telling my parents that I didn't know how to slow dance.

Though honestly, when could I have possibly learned such a skill?

I'd never been to a dance in my life, just a family wedding once when I was six. During the reception I only focused on stuffing as much cake into my face as I could, and I didn't pay attention to the dance floor.

"OK. Here's the deal. I don't know how to slow dance, and I'm thinking I should know *before* the dance," I finished lamely.

There it was.

My Non-Slow-Dancer Status was now on display for the world (OK, my parents) to see.

"Oh, is that all? That's easy," my mom said, and she jumped up and grabbed my hand.

"Wait. Why don't you and Dad model it for me, and then I can try," I said hoping to postpone the humiliation of learning to slow dance with my MOM for a few seconds longer.

"Why, I'd be delighted to dance with this beautiful young lady," my dad said, and he got up to turn on some slow music.

After he found a song he liked (the seventies called, they want their music back!), he bowed low in front of mom.

She giggled and took his hand, and they started a slow shuffle in time to the song.

Watching the two of them, it looked pretty simple.

Boy put hands on Girl's hips and Girl put hands on Boy's shoulders. Boy stands about a foot apart from Girl, and then both Boy and Girl do a kind of circle/shuffle to the beat.

My mom put her head on my dad's shoulder, and I told her to stop. I was trying to keep this as realistic as possible and there was no way on earth that Harper was going to put her head on my shoulder unless she fainted.

They danced for about a minute, and after watching, I was pretty sure I knew how it should go.

Now it was my turn.

I put my hands on my mom's waist as far from her butt as I could get. That was too creepy to even think about. My dad put a new song on the stereo, and I kind of shuffled with her and tried to avoid stepping on her toes.

"Keep those hands where I can see them, Jack!" my dad joked.

"Dad, don't make me barf!" I yelled back, not caring if I offended my mom.

As we did the circle-shuffle in the living room, I felt pretty confident in my slow-dance skills Of course, I was a lot less confident in my asking-Harper-to-slow-dance skills.

The song ended and I quickly dropped my hands from my mom's waist.

"Not bad, Jack," she said. "You only stepped on my toes twice."

"Sorry," I said as I looked down at my apparently two left feet.

"So what about fast dancing, Jack? You know I used to own the dance floor back in the day," my dad said as he fiddled with the stereo yet again.

"Um, no, I got that covered," I said as loud techno music began blasting from the speakers.

"Nah, come on. Let me teach you some patented Par-ker dance moves," he said as he flapped his arms up and down like a prehistoric bird. My mom decided to join in, and she started some weird hip shaking that also involved little kicks of her feet.

If the neighbors could see in the window, they would think both of them were having a seizure and call an ambulance.

I looked at the two of them flailing around like chickens on fire and decided that if dancing skills were hereditary, then I was doomed.

CHAPTER TWENTY-THREE

The next morning at school was pretty average. The only interesting thing was news from Xin that he'd seen Leo's dad mowing the lawn, which was apparently something he hadn't done in a while. Xin also said he saw Mr. Delaney leaving the house the night before, which again hadn't happened lately. Hopefully he was going to see about the job with Harper's stepdad.

Maybe having a job would at least keep Mr. Delaney out of Leo's way, and maybe Mrs. Delaney wouldn't have to keep working three jobs. I knew it wasn't a permanent solution for Leo's problem, but it was a start, and I felt good about my small part in it.

All we could talk about during lunch was the dance and Bryce's FunRun competition. He didn't talk about it, but I thought he was listening.

"I think it would be so great for Bryce to win so that Feathers would see we really do belong with the other kids," Harper said as we ate lunch in SPED-land.

"You still don't get it," Xin told her. "He only wants us locked away in here so that when the state test time comes around, the Huge All-Important State Test, then the stupid SPED-ers don't take it and pull his scores down."

"Don't say stupid, Xin," Ms. McFee corrected him. Though she didn't disagree with anything else Xin was saying.

"He's obsessed with being the highest ranking middle school in the state," Xin went on. "And if he has to lock us up in here to do it, oh well."

Again, McFee didn't tell him to hush like she usually did when we complained about this. I wondered if maybe she was changing her mind about where SPED kids belonged.

Our afternoon was spent on boring American History and even more boring grammar exercises. We'd moved on from pronouns to something called gerunds, which were verbs ending in –ing that act like nouns (!?!).

I pretty much wanted to kill whoever thought of such craziness.

Wait.

Killing is wrong.

The gerund in my sentence is killing! Maybe I got this after all.

At 3:30 the loudspeaker finally crackled to life, and Principal Feathers came on the air.

"Good afternoon, Hickory Hills. We only have a few announcements today. Pottery club meets next Monday after school in Ms. Milkin's room. The school wrestling team has an informational meeting scheduled for next Wednesday in Coach Kilwicki's office."

Feathers paused to get his breath, and then he continued.

"And of course, Hickory Hills, tomorrow's the big day! Our Fall Festival will be happening tomorrow evening at six o'clock. There'll be a professional DJ for the dance, food and drinks to purchase, and of course the festivities begin with our FunRun to see which homeroom has the best athlete."

We all looked at Bryce, and Xin reached over and gave him a high five. Bryce actually held up his huge paw for the slap.

"Now, bus riders, you're dismissed," Feathers finally finished.

A swarm of kids poured into the halls, and Bernie and Leo and I all walked together to the buses.

We were talking about how the FunRun might be set up and what sort of obstacles they would have when, out of nowhere, Colin and his posse of hyenas surrounded us. Leo shrunk into himself, but Bernie got an aggressive look in her eyes.

"Hey, dummies. No teachers here to protect you now, are there?" Colin said.

"I don't need no teacher around for protection. Though you might when I get through with your scrawny ass," Bernie said in an instant. She never failed to take it from zero to sixty in about a second.

"Is that right?" Colin said and shifted from one foot to another. He looked at Leo and me. "So you idiots gonna let a girl protect you?"

I didn't know what to say to that, but I didn't have time as Bernie jumped in again. "I told you once, you're the one who's gonna need protection if you don't get the hell outta our way."

You got to hand it to Bernie. She didn't back down. I guess forty-four houses in thirteen years makes you tough or kills you. And Bernie sure ain't dead.

And neither was I.

I didn't know if it was the excitement of the dance or knowing that my dad had my back on getting out of SGS or just some random hormones floating through my brain. But whatever it was, I'd decided to stand up for myself. A little bit, anyway.

"Yeah, get outta our way, Colin," I said copying Bernie's words, and the whole group looked at me in surprise. I was surprised myself and definitely a little nervous.

"Shut it, Parker. I don't want to get in trouble for fighting at school, you moron. I just wanted to tell you SPED heads that I'm winning the FunRun tomorrow. My dad's practically paying for this stupid dance, and I better win the obstacle course," Colin said.

"Hmph," Bernie said giving him a dirty look. "We'll see about that, won't we?"

"I know that you guys probably chose Bryce as your rep since he's so big he should already be in high school," Colin looked at his friends and laughed. "He's just too stupid to get there!" he added.

Colin's idiot friends laughed along like the robots they were, but Bernie wasn't laughing.

"Good one. I'll tell Bryce you said he's stupid next time I see him," she said.

Colin looked a little nervous at that but kept a brave front.

"Fine. Tell the loser SPED head all about it. Also tell him that he better not win tomorrow or Leo will pay the price," Colin said.

Bernie looked at him through narrowed eyes, and I thought she was going to bust his nose for that comment. Luckily for Colin, another wave of kids came down the hall toward the buses and poured between our group and Colin's.

I took that as a chance to get Bernie moving and tugged at her arm while Colin and his crew walked in the opposite direction towards the front of the school. He turned around one last time as he walked away and yelled, "Remember who wins tomorrow!"

"I do believe Mr. Markus is a bit nervous about his competition," Bernie said with a grin on her face as we made our way to the bus lanes.

"Whew. I really don't like that guy," I said as I tried not to freak out about the fact that I'd just stood up for myself to one of the school's biggest bullies.

"Good job stepping up, Jack," Bernie said and Leo nodded.

"I just said what you said," I admitted.

"But the more people who push back against the Colins of the world, the better," she said and looked over at Leo.

"Don't worry, Leo. I won't let them bother you," Bernie said we stood in the bus lanes.

"I know. He's all talk now, I think," Leo said.

"Yep. He can push around weak kids or younger ones, but anyone stands up to him and he crumples like a tissue," Bernie said as she walked to her bus.

"And this girl gonna blow her nose on that tissue before it's all over with," she added with a laugh.

CHAPTER TWENTY-FOUR

The big day had finally arrived, and on Friday morning, the SPED crew was so excited that we were bouncing off the walls.

Literally.

Before the morning announcements, Skeever had been showing us a dance move, and he bounced off of McFee's front wall and bumped his head on her desk. Ouch.

We hadn't seen this much excitement at school since the lizards escaped from Mr. Browning's science classroom last year and Mrs. Magilly had gone screaming down the hall in terror.

Good times.

No one was absent since you couldn't do an after school activity if you weren't actually at school that day. I prayed that McFee would lay off the gerunds for the day, and thankfully my prayers were answered. She always wrote the day's lessons and activities on the board so that we knew what to expect, and I didn't see the first sign of grammar up there. Hurray!

She was actually taking it super easy on us with both a video AND journal time. Videos just required you to not fall asleep or drool on yourself, and journal time was when we took out these little composition books and wrote about whatever we wanted. Between those two things and lunch, that would almost be the whole day!

Principal Loser was finishing the announcements with his MegaLame Probably Patented Slogan "make it a great day or not...the choice is yours" when we all randomly said the last four words with him. All six of us (Bryce just watched) practically shouted "The Choice Is Yours!" and then we all burst out laughing.

This was definitely going to be a good day.

McFee was startled at our yelling, but then she laughed along with us.

"Ms. McFee, are you going to the dance tonight?" Leo asked her.

"Of course, Leo. The teachers have to chaperone the dance."

"Oh great! I'll be the only one there with a parent...I mean a foster parent," Bernie said with a smile.

We all stared at her in confusion, but Harper understood immediately.

"That's great, Bernie!! I'm so happy for you guys!" she said and ran over to give Bernie a huge hug.

"Can someone please tell me why Harper is happy?" Skeever asked.

"I wasn't going to tell you guys til it was 100% certain, but it's 98% certain, so what the heck. I'm going to be Bernie's foster mom for now, and hopefully her adopted mom someday," Ms. McFee explained.

The entire class jumped up and surrounded Bernie to give her hugs or high fives. Even Bryce came over and gave Bernie a bear hug that could've squished her flat.

Leo was grinning like a crazy man. This meant his friend and guardian angel didn't have to go away, and that had to be a huge relief in more ways than one.

"No more changing schools or changing houses every five minutes. No more going to a new place without knowing what kind of people I'm heading for. McFee knows I'm kind of crazy, and for some reason, she doesn't mind!" Bernie said.

"So how cool is it to have your mom as your teacher? You'll have easy access to all the answer keys for tests!" Xin said laughing.

"Not so fast. All tests and answers are off limits," Ms. McFee said as she moved towards the VCR and began getting ready to show the video.

Before she pressed play, she turned and looked at all of us.

"Though I did want to tell you that now Bernie is settled, I can speak up to Principal Feathers a little more about getting you out of SGS for high school. I couldn't before since I needed a reference from him when I went in front of the foster parent people," she finished.

That made perfect sense and I felt bad for doubting that McFee had our backs.

"Thanks, Ms. McFee. We appreciate everything you do for us," Skeever said.

"Suck Up!" I shouted and we all laughed again.

"Let's get started, people," McFee continued, and she pressed play.

I couldn't help but smile in the darkened classroom. Bernie had a home. Leo's dad had a job. I had a shot at getting out of SGS.

Now if I could just get a dance...

That got me to thinking, and I realized that I probably wasn't the only one at school who was nervous about asking a girl to dance tonight. Though maybe I'd be the only one asking Harper.

Just then she laughed at a joke from Skeever and I looked over at her.

The only one asking *her* to dance? Ha! Not hardly.

She was so pretty that there'd be a line of anxious, sweaty boys hoping for a dance, and somehow I had to be one of them.

We finally made it through the day, and Feathers didn't torture everyone with long announcements that afternoon. He just dismissed the bus riders and said he hoped to see us all at the dance tonight

I wanted to hurry to the buses to avoid seeing Colin and Company again, but Leo and Bernie were strolling slowly so I stayed with them.

"So when do you get to move into Ms. McFee's place?" Leo asked.

"Sometime next week. My current foster folks acted like they were sad I was leaving, but I know they're glad. They wanted a cute little kid, and they got me instead."

"Oh, stop. You're plenty cute. You just have a mouth on you," I said.

"Oh, so now you're going after me too, Mr. Flirty Jack? Goldilocks will be mad if you're two-timing her!" Bernie said with a laugh.

"You know what I mean..."

"Just messing with you. Now you know you gotta ask Harper to dance tonight, right? She'll be hurt if you don't."

"Yeah, right. Harper thinks of me as her lame cousin or maybe her awkward kid brother. We're 'just friends,' remember?" I said as I walked towards the bus.

"Don't be too sure about that, Jack, see you tonight!" Bernie said as she climbed up her bus steps.

"Yeah, Jack," Leo added as he headed to his bus. "I really do think she likes you."

I kept walking by myself to my bus, and after I found a seat I barely noticed the cute girls as they walked down the center aisle. I guess seeing a real girl in class every day had made me not notice other girls as much. As the bus rolled home, I thought about what Leo and Bernie had said about Harper liking me, but I knew they were wrong. We were definitely "just friends."

When I got home, I grabbed the mail out of the box and walked in the front door. On the top of the stack was a letter addressed to my dad from the Nelson County Board of Education.

Wow! The school board wrote him back!

I called him immediately.

"Hey JackaRack, what's up? Ready for your big dance debut tonight?" he said after just one ring.

"Hi, Dad. Yeah, sure. Ready to rock out," I answered. "Listen Dad, you got a letter from the school board."

"Great, son. Open it up! Whatever they have to say is your business a lot more than mine," he said.

Gotta love my dad.

My mom would want to read it first, see if there was any bad news and then try and tell me the bad news in a good way.

I ripped open the envelope and saw the school board logo at the top. I scanned the two short paragraphs and let out a sigh of disappointment.

"What is it Jack? What did they say?" my dad asked from far away.

"They say that they appreciate your concern, but that the decisions about classroom arrangements are made by the local school principals and they don't interfere. In other words, Feathers gets all the say so."

"Bummer," my dad said.

"Yeah. Big bummer," I answered quietly.

"Well, I'm not giving up. I'll make an appointment to talk to the principal."

"That's what McFee said, but he'll never budge, Dad. He wants his perfect scores on the state tests. Unless we get a new principal, the SPED group will always be separate," I said sadly. "And unless we can get into regular classes this year, then high school will be four more years of the same thing and no college hopes at all."

The thought of four years in a small room with the same six kids made me want to drop out of high school before I'd even started.

"I'm really sorry, Jack," my dad said.

"Not your fault you have a stupid kid," I answered.

"Jack, you're not st..."

I cut him off. "Thanks, Dad. I gotta go get ready for the dance," I said and hung up without even waiting for a goodbye.

After that depressing news, I didn't feel like having my usual after-school snack, so I went straight to the living room and flopped down on the couch.

So four more years of small group, no college and a future in a paint store.

Who wouldn't want to celebrate news like that?

CHAPTER TWENTY-FIVE

My parents were closing the store a little early to get home in time to drive me to the dance, and I didn't look forward to my mom wanting to comb my hair for me or wash behind my ears or something.

I changed out of my T-shirt and put on a polo shirt. When we'd bought it, my mom had said that the blue color "brought out my eyes." I'm not sure what she meant by that, but it looked pretty good.

At a quarter of six, my folks pulled into the driveway and my mom came in the house in a rush.

"Jack, Jack," she screamed from the front door.

Since I was sitting on the couch two feet from her, I really didn't understand her need to yell.

"Right here, Mom," I said and she jumped three feet in the air.

"Oh my goodness! You scared me!"

"Sorry, but I don't know why you're so nervous," I said as I stood up and smoothed my shirt out a bit.

"Don't you look handsome!" she said, trying to comb my hair before I ducked away from her.

"Thanks, Mom. Can we go?"

"Sure, honey. Your dad's waiting in the car, but I want some pictures before we go."

"Mom!! It's just a stupid school dance. No pictures," I said in annoyance.

"But it's your first school dance, and there's only one first."

I knew she'd win and arguing would just take time, so I agreed and she grabbed her camera. She could have her pictures, but I didn't have to smile. No way was I having a photographic record of my metal mouth.

After the photo shoot (say cheese!) we walked out the front door and one of the neighbors was outside watering her flowers. Of course my mom couldn't resist.

"Hi Brenda," she yelled across the yard. "Doesn't Jack look handsome? He's going to his first school dance tonight, and his dad and I taught him to slow dance."

I wondered if they made Mom Muzzles and decided I should probably invent one as this was only going to get worse.

I ducked into the minivan to get away from my embarrassing mother, but now it was my dad's turn.

"Whoa, JackAttack!" he said and turned around from the front seat. "Looking like a Lady Killer if I ever saw one!"

Seriously? I was a skinny middle schooler in a blue polo shirt, and these two were acting like I was the new Justin Bieber.

"Thanks, Dad."

"You look great! Harper will want to dance with you for sure when she sees you in that shirt," Dad added as he buckled his seat belt back up.

My mom opened the door and was getting in. "She sure will, but don't let her get too forward. Girls can be so pushy these days! Mrs. Rice at the store was telling me about girls who text her son Matthew at all hours."

Matthew was the most popular jock at HHMS, the quarterback of the football team, and literally at the top of the Social Ladder—ahead of all the Colins and Britneys combined.

To hear my mom comparing me to him was worse than depressing; it was delusional.

"I won't let anyone get forward or backward, Mom. Can we just go, please? I don't want to miss Bryce in the FunRun," I said as I looked straight ahead.

"Sure, honey. Now we'll be there promptly at 8:30 to pick you up."

"OK," I said and wondered if two and a half hours of Dance Fun might be a bit much.

"Though if you want to leave early just call us," Mom added.

Ahhhhh!!! Get outta my head, Mom! I sometimes worried that she could read my thoughts, and times like this made me wonder.

"I won't leave early," I said just to throw her off.

We were at the school in a few minutes, and balloons lined the front driveway and parking lot. Carfuls of kids were being dropped off.

There were Spazzy sixth graders who didn't care how silly they looked. Awkward seventh graders trying not to look excited, but who secretly wanted to act like Spazzy sixth graders. And of course the SuperCool eighth graders who were trying to look like the whole thing was a bore.

I knew better. The eighth graders were just as excited as the sixth graders, but for a whole different reason. Sixth graders may not want to slow dance with one another, but the eighth graders couldn't wait. I still didn't know if I'd get up the courage to ask Harper to dance, but it would be fun to see who else coupled up.

Our car finally got to the front of the school, and I climbed out and waved goodbye to my annoying parents. I shut the door fast before my mom could say something embarrassing or tell me to eat only healthy snacks.

After they drove off, I took a deep breath and was only slightly-severely nervous.

Standing alone on the sidewalk, I realized that it would've been a great idea to plan on meeting a couple of the SPED-ers at the door so I wouldn't have to go in alone. I looked around at the crowd of kids and realized that I didn't know most of the students at this school.

If they didn't ride my bus (twenty-four kids) or sit in my class (six kids) then I was clueless about who anyone was. Thinking about that fact made me even more aggravated with Principal Feathers and his isolation theory.

Just then Xin and Leo got out of Xin's car, and I was saved the embarrassment of walking into the school alone. Both of them had actually cleaned up a little bit and I thought I caught a whiff of cologne on Xin. Good touch. We exchanged high fives and nervous smiles.

"Let's get this party started," Xin said as we headed into the school.

The balloons continued through the halls and towards the gym where the FunRun and the dance were happening. We joined the stream of excited kids heading that way, and I thought I saw Bryce's tall head sticking out of the crowd.

"Man I hope Bryce can beat Colin in the FunRun," Xin said as we moved with the herd down the hallway.

"I just hope *someone* beats him," Leo agreed, and I thought maybe Matthew Rice had a shot.

When we got in the gym, I could see the huge inflatable obstacle course that the FunRun participants would finish up on. According to Xinho, all thirty contestants had to first do five laps around the gym, climb the ropes on the challenge course, touch the ceiling, come down the rope, and then scramble over the inflatable mountain in front of us.

I stared up at the dangling ropes on the challenge course that hung all the way from the ceiling to the floor. They looked like thick, leafless vines and I wondered how anyone could get up and down one of those monsters.

The room was buzzing as kids continued to pour into the doors, and Feathers took the microphone from the DJ. We heard his nasal whine.

"Students. Attention, quiet, attention," he said as he attempted to silence the rowdy group. "All contestants in the FunRun need to walk carefully to the far end of the gym."

Ignoring the "walk carefully" part, I saw a variety of kids as they scrambled over to the starting line. Some hopped around in nervousness while others stretched and looked like they were getting ready to run a marathon.

Of course it really wasn't too fair having an eighth grader compete against a sixth grader, but no one really expected a sixth grader to actually win. Winning something like this was more of an eighth-grade privilege, and the whole thing was just for fun anyway.

Unless you were Colin.

I saw him in the group of runners, and he looked as cocky as ever. I guess he thought his dad could buy a win for him, too. Bryce was there, but he stood away from the crowd of kids, and it was hard to tell what he might be thinking.

"Now students, the rules are very simple. You run five laps around the gym, then climb up those ropes," Feathers said.

When he said that, every head looked up at the ropes. No way could I ever even think about getting up one of those, and I was super glad the SPED-ers had Bryce to represent for us.

"After the ropes comes the inflatable course," Feathers went on and again everyone turned to look at the huge vinyl mountain.

Now that part looked kind of fun, but not in front of the whole school.

"And the first one out of the obstacle course wins! Now runners, all of you get to the starting line," Feathers finally finished.

Looking over at the group, we saw that while they would be a mass of runners at first, the fastest ones would pull away quickly. The top five or so would be the ones who made it interesting.

The DJ, courtesy of Colin's dad, was playing "Eye of the Tiger" in an attempt to pump the runners up, and seeing the DJ reminded me of the whole reason that we were really here. Looking around the semi-dark gym, I hoped that he played more slow songs than fast ones.

Surely at *some* point I could get up enough courage to ask Harper to dance to *some* kind of song.

I realized that I hadn't seen her yet. She was probably being "Fashionably Late."

"I guess Harper is too cool to show up on time," I said to Xin.

"Yeah, I thought she'd be here to cheer for Bryce," Leo said.

"Oh well, her loss," I added.

Xin and Leo and I were all crowded in the middle of the gym floor with the rest of HHMS as the runners took their marks. I saw a good mixture of boys (including Matthew Rice Star Quarterback) and girls preparing to run, and of course Colin and Bryce. What I wouldn't give for someone, anyone, to beat that smirk off of Colin's face!

Principal Feather had the mic up to his mouth again. "Runners, take your places," he said, and the sound echoed from the speakers.

All thirty of the homeroom reps stood at the starting line.

"On your mark, get set, GO!" Feathers shouted into the microphone.

The sound of thirty clomping sets of tennis shoes could barely be heard over the screaming of six hundred kids. We all stood in the center of the gym, and the runners raced around the edges. It was obvious very quickly who the fastest kids were, and both Colin and Bryce were in that first group.

Every kid was cheering for their classmate, and even though there were only seven kids in our class, I thought we were doing a great job of cheering Bryce on. I could see that McFee and Bernie had come into the gym and were both yelling their heads off.

The group did the first three laps pretty quickly, but after that the pace slowed down a bit. At the end of lap four, Bryce and Colin and two other kids – a sixth grade girl by the looks of her and another eighth grade boy who rides my bus – were leading the pack in a pretty even run. Matthew Rice had twisted an ankle or something and was limping towards Coach Kilwicki, the gym teacher.

"Hey, Matthew Rice is out!" I told Xin when I saw Matthew struggling off the course.

"That's good for Bryce," Xin said, and we went back to watching the runners.

By the time they finished the five laps and got to the ropes, there were only four students that even stood a chance. Some of the other kids had even stopped running when they realized that they could never catch the leaders before they made it to the ropes.

Since there were only five ropes, the first kids to make it through the laps and get there had a huge advantage.

From where I stood, the ropes looked like threads hanging from the ceiling, and I could only imagine how awful it would be to have to climb them with the whole school watching.

Bryce didn't seem to care who was watching and he looked like a robot as he ran. He hardly looked tired after he finished his last lap and headed to the ropes. Colin was right behind him, but he looked like he might puke at any time.

Xin poked me in the side, "Bryce has this!" he said excitedly.

"I sure hope so!" Leo added.

The entire school was still screaming and clapping, but now all heads were craned up to watch the kids climbing. Bryce was big, but he must have had some great upper body strength as he kept putting one hand over the other and heading straight up. Colin used his legs more, but was still scrambling up fast.

The sixth grade girl who had been one of the fast runners went about four feet up a rope and then fell back down. Now it was just the three eighth-grade boys.

I looked over at the gym doorway for a second and noticed that Harper was there with Britney and her crew. Harper looked really pretty, and I knew in that second I'd never get up the courage to ask her to dance.

Leo said, "Look!" and I whipped my head back in time to see Bryce coming down the rope at about a zillion miles an hour. How he did that without frying his hands, I couldn't imagine. Colin had just touched the roof when he saw that Bryce was nearly halfway down the rope, so Colin started coming down hand over hand nearly as fast as Bryce had done. The third eighth grader had bailed after ten feet of rope, so it was down to just the two boys.

SPED versus CREEP. We had to win this!

I looked at the big inflatable obstacle course and saw a climbing section first, followed by a slide, and then these weird blown up barriers that you had to climb through with a tunnel at the end. We wouldn't be able to see inside once Bryce and Colin got over the climbing section.

Both boys set out at a full sprint towards the final obstacle and Colin had the lead, by just a little, for the first time in the race. I thought I saw fear on Colin's face and he kept turning his head to check on Bryce. Bryce just looked straight ahead though and didn't seem to notice Colin at all.

Someone in the crowd began chanting "Bryce, Bryce, Bryce" and soon 95 percent of the school was screaming for Bryce to win.

I guess when you bully most of the kids at school, the only ones who will cheer for you are the few you don't mess with. The Colin supporters were easily drowned out.

Both boys reached the inflatable at almost the same moment. Bryce leaped onto it with a big jump and was nearly over the top while Colin was desperately trying to scramble up the slippery side.

I looked over at the DJ table where Principal Feathers was standing with Colin's dad. Feathers looked a little nervous, and Mr. Markus looked plenty mad that his son was not in the lead.

I guess money doesn't buy everything after all.

After they climbed up the inflatable wall, there was a slide that Colin and Bryce had to flop down, and then the tunnel that was filled with who knew what. Once both boys got into the tunnel, the crowd got quiet as they pushed their way through the huge vinyl monster.

Just when the entire school was starting to wonder whether either boy would come out of the inflatable fiend, Bryce threw himself out of the end of the tunnel, sprang to his feet, and crossed the finish line.

"He did it!" Xin screamed.

"SPEDs rule! Douchebags drool!" Skeever began chanting til a teacher gave him a dirty look.

The entire school had erupted in a massive cheer, and the SPED-heads, McFee included, ran over and hugged Bryce. I'm not sure if he hugged us back, but he didn't stop us either.

"Way to go, Bryce! You smoked his butt" Bernie said.

"Great job, Bryce," McFee agreed, and we all high fived our way around the circle while the whole school clapped and yelled.

Colin climbed weakly out of the obstacle course a good ten seconds after Bryce finished and started limping away towards his dad. He was pointing to his foot and probably coming up with some excuse about why he didn't win.

It seemed like everyone was congratulating Bryce, and I think I actually saw him smile a little bit. It felt weird to be noticed and congratulated by everyone since they all knew we were Bryce's classmates, and somehow that made us cool by association.

It might just have been for one night, for a moment, but it felt good to finally be a part of that school.

CHAPTER TWENTY-SIX

After the race finished, the coaches quickly deflated the obstacle course and dragged it into a supply closet. I guess they didn't want us kids messing around on it.

Principal Feathers congratulated Bryce but didn't seem too happy that he won. Maybe that's because Colin's dad was standing right next to him when he gave Bryce his trophy.

Oh well. Better luck next time, Loser.

That felt pretty good. Calling Colin a Loser instead of the other way around.

The DJ had started playing music, and I could see kids already shaking it on the dance floor.

As I saw a boy dance from the back, his butt looked like a bobble head—and that made me wonder what the heck I looked like from the back. The back of Jack was something I hadn't considered when I'd studied my dancing reflection in the mirror.

Did my butt look weird? Did the back of my head bob up and down like a yo-yo? I had a mental picture of people laughing and pointing at my back while I tried to dance, and I knew I had to see what I looked like from behind.

I decided it might not be a bad idea for one more practice run in the boys' bathroom before I actually went out on the dance floor. I figured I could stand in front of the mirror and try to look over my shoulder to see what I looked like from behind.

Then an even better idea hit me.

What if I used my phone to record my dancing from behind and then watched it back to make sure that I wasn't too spazzmo on the floor?

Brilliant!

Why I didn't think of taping myself when I was at Xin's house, I didn't know.

I looked around for Xin so he could record me in the hallway, but he was already talking to some girls. Dang, he was quick!

Leo was my next choice, but he was in the middle of Skeever and Bernie, so I didn't ask him because I could only imagine what Bernie would say.

That left Harper. Never.

Or Bryce. Maybe.

Bryce would never tell anyone since he didn't talk, and he'd never been mean or anything, so I doubt if he'd think I was too pitiful. Or if he thought it, at least he wouldn't say it.

He was still standing over by the DJ table holding his FunRun trophy, so I decided what the heck and walked over to him.

"Hey Bryce, great job on the FunRun," I said.

He just nodded.

"Listen. I have a favor to ask," I went on.

He nodded again.

"Would you mind coming into the hall and recording me dancing from the back so I can make sure I don't look too mental?" I said and waited for his response.

He nodded again, put down his trophy, and began walking into the hallway.

Wow! That was easy.

We quickly slipped out into the back hallway where we could still hear the music but no one would see us. Now I was feeling super goofy for going this far to see if I was a terrible dancer, but Bryce didn't seem to think that there was anything wrong with the idea.

"Here's my phone. You just press the red button here to shoot," I said handing my phone to Bryce.

"Thanks again. I know this is stupid, but I just don't want to look like a spaz out there," I continued. "Or at least too much of a spaz!"

Bryce just nodded (again) and took the phone from me.

I had my back to him and had just started dancing when the door to the gym opened.

"What are you doing out here?" I jumped when I heard Feathers' voice and stopped dancing immediately.

"Um...just getting some air. Bryce was tired after his big race," I said quickly.

"Well there's no supervision out here, so you need to get back inside," he said and looked at Bryce with a strange expression on his face. "Tired after the race, huh? What a shame. I knew I shouldn't have let you retards participate in the FunRun. Mr. Markus is furious that Colin lost."

I stood there openmouthed in shock that my *principal* had just used the word "retard." That word had been banned since second grade when Marty Smith yelled it on the playground and got in big trouble from Mrs. Cummings.

"What?" Feathers said with a cruel smile on his face. "Don't like hearing the truth? You're a room full of dummies and I shouldn't have let you come to my dance, much less participate in the FunRun."

I was shocked that he was saying such awful things, but figured if he was being so honest, then here was my chance to hear from Feathers himself why he wouldn't let us into regular classes. Bryce had put himself out there to represent for the SPED-ers, so it was my turn to do the same.

"Yeah, we're retards all right, and that's why you keep us locked up, You can't let the idiots take your special state tests. Can't let them bring your scores down from a 100 to maybe a 96?" I said, feeling nervous but not wanting to show it.

"Maybe you're not so dumb after all," Feathers said as he looked me up and down. "Yes. My reputation as a principal was built on our school making the top scores in the state, and if that means keeping you dummies in a special class, then that's what I'll do."

"But you know that if we don't get in regular classes in middle school, we can't get in them in high school either? We're stuck in SGS and you can forget about college."

"You're stuck where you belong," Feathers said. "Boys like this one"—he pointed at Bryce—"have no place with normal kids. Even if he can run fast," he finished.

"I told my mom you were a terrible principal and she didn't believe me. She will now," I said to Feathers.

"Oh, please. You won't even bother telling mommy and daddy about this conversation. Why would you?" he said as he turned to open the door into the gym. "This one never talks," he said pointing at Bryce. "And no one will believe a boy who can't even keep his letters straight," he said with a laugh.

"Now get back inside before I give you both detention for being out in the hall without permission," he continued and walked to the door and held it open.

This couldn't be happening. I knew that Feathers was an idiot, but to limit the chances of all the SPED kids just to make himself look good? I couldn't believe anyone could be that selfish.

My first thought was to tell Ms. McFee, but maybe Feathers was right. Who would believe me? He'd deny it and it would look like I was still whining about getting out of SGS.

Bryce walked back into the gym, and I followed him in a kind of daze. Feathers closed the door and came in behind us. He looked the same as ever and no one would ever believe the horrible things he'd just said to us.

My face felt hot and my stomach was sick. Feathers had ruined this night for me. When you thought about it, he'd ruined middle school for me and all the other Small Group kids.

I wanted to leave and forget all of this, but it was still two hours til my folks came to get me. I realized I could call them to come get me early, but then I also realized that Bryce still had my phone.

I turned to ask him for it back but saw that he'd already walked over to the DJ table.

He was leaning over and talking – wait, BRYCE WAS TALKING? – to the DJ.

Both Bryce and the DJ were huddled around the screen of my phone watching something, and I was terrified that Bryce was showing the DJ my lame dance moves.

I sprinted straight over to them in a panic. I had to get my phone back before everyone saw how pathetic I was.

"Jeez Bryce. What are you doing? Give me my phone!" I said angrily and put my hand out to collect it.

"Cool it, kid. Your buddy here has something interesting," the DJ said.

"Yeah, me making a fool of myself! Now give me my phone back!"

"Hold on, man. You're not the one acting the fool," the DJ said as he paused the music.

The music came to an abrupt stop and so did all the chatter from the students as they wondered why the music was off. The DJ held my phone in one hand and his microphone in the other.

Was he going to play the recording of me dancing? No one could see it from far away, but maybe he was going to do a play by play of my lame moves!

This whole night had become a nightmare. I should've never come to this stupid dance...I should've stayed home safe in my Friday night bubble with my parents.

I'd be alone in the bubble, but at least I wouldn't be humiliated in front of the whole school!

"Hey Hickory Hills!! Wuzzzzuuuuupppp? Are you having a good time??" the DJ began.

The crowd roared back at him with a huge "YEAH!"

"Awesome. Now my man Bryce here, amazing win at the FunRun by the way, dude, has something special he'd like to play for you peeps. Something that his friend Jack did that I know you'll all be interested in."

My heart was pounding out of my chest and I tried to think of something to stop this. Why was Bryce showing my dance tape? What had I ever done to him except help him with math problems?

I honestly thought I was going to barf right on the gym floor, and I wanted to make a run for it. But if I ran out now, then I wouldn't know how bad the damage was. I couldn't move.

I looked at the curious faces of the whole school as they stared at Bryce and the DJ. How could I stop this?

"What's up with Bryce?" Leo said as he and Bernie came up behind me.

"Yeah. I swear I just saw him talking to the DJ." Bernie said.

"He's about to ruin my life!" I said, and they both looked at me like I was nuts.

Just then the DJ held the mic up to my phone and Bryce pressed play. You could hear the dance music in the background, but from where I was I couldn't see anything on the small screen.

Wanting to disappear on the spot, I was trying to think of a good reason to tell people when they asked about the stupid recording of me dancing when I heard Feathers' voice. "I knew I shouldn't have let you retards participate in the FunRun. Mr. Markus is furious that Colin lost." The recording of our principal played loud and clear on the DJ's sound system.

Next came my voice and it was weird to hear myself on the loud speakers, "But you know that if we don't get in regular classes in middle school, we can't get in them in high school either? We're stuck in SGS and you can forget about college."

"You're stuck where you belong," the recording went on.

The DJ stopped the recording here, but the whole school had heard what our principal really thought about the SPED kids.

Feathers had already started hustling over to the DJ table with a look of horror on his face, but the damage was done. The students began buzzing as the tape continued.

McFee went straight to Feathers as he stood there trying to get his hands on the phone.

"Give me that phone!" Feathers said.

"I'm pretty sure that phone belongs to Jack. I'm also pretty sure that the school board might want to hear that recording again," McFee said.

Bernie leaned over and gave me a high five. "Nice work, Sherlock. Never would've thought to tape him talking trash," she said.

"It wasn't my idea. It was Bryce!" I told her.

"Dude! You're the Man!" Xin said when he came into the group and they all acted like I was some kind of miracle worker.

"It seriously was all Bryce," I tried to tell them, but no one was listening.

Things got even weirder when I noticed that Bryce had taken the microphone from the DJ's hand. He cleared his throat and it sounded like a door that was stuck and needed oil.

"I think my man Bryce has an announcement for y'all," the DJ said, leaning into the microphone.

The school got quiet and even Feathers and McFee quit arguing and looked up. No one wanted to miss Bryce making an announcement.

"Principal Feathers," Bryce began quietly.

It was so weird to hear him talking!

"Make it a great *career* or not, the choice is yours!" he finished with a small smile.

The students all erupted into laughter, and the DJ cranked the music back up to full blast. Kids were freaking out and the entire gym was buzzing about Feathers and his horrible remarks. I saw the teachers talking behind their hands to one another and shaking their heads.

Lots of kids were coming up to me and saying stuff like "Way to go, Jack!" and "Good job, Parker!" It was super weird to go from invisible shadow to celebrity status in just a minute, and I wasn't sure if I liked it or not.

I saw Mr. Markus standing by Feathers, and even he looked mad. McFee was still chewing on him and looked like she was going to take his head off.

My brain was on overload, and I still felt strange after the panic I'd had when I thought Bryce was showing everyone the recording of me dancing.

Time for a break.

I made it to the line for drinks and got a glass of soda when I realized that Harper was standing behind me.

"Hey Jack, way to go! I didn't think it was your style to fight back," she said giving me a big hug.

"It wasn't me. It was Bryce," I answered honestly, not really even registering the fact that Harper had hugged me.

"But you were brave enough to ask Feathers the question in the first place, so I think you both qualify as my heroes right now."

Zero to Hero. Definitely a Disney movie.

"Um, well. Cool. Thanks," I muttered wondering when I'd return to Zero status.

"This will get us out of SGS for sure," she went on.

Out of SGS?

Out of SGS and into different classrooms instead of just one tiny closet?

Out of SGS and into classes with different teachers and new faces instead of the same people every day?

Out of SGS with no bullies and just us SPED-ers?

Now that getting out of SGS looked like something that could actually happen instead of a crazy dream, I started to panic. How was I going to keep up in regular class? How was I going to fit in? How was I going to read what everyone else was reading?

I knew McFee wouldn't desert me, but the thought of going into mainstream classes was freaking me out already.

Harper just stood there with a smile on her face.

"It's a good thing, Jack," Harper said. "You'll see."

I realized that the rush of doubts flooding my brain was my mom talking, and I tried to calm down and shut out her "glass half empty" voice.

Then I pictured myself in regular classes here and in high school.

New faces. New friends. New future.

Wasn't that what I was after all along?

So while leaving SGS was scary, it was necessary. It was kind of like taking the training wheels off your bike. You might hit the concrete a couple of times, but at least you could go fast when you were ready.

The DJ was blasting his music, so when Harper asked me to dance, I wasn't really sure what she was saying. I just went along when she grabbed my hand and led me to the dance floor.

On the way, Britney stopped her and whispered in her ear. I could tell from the look on her face that Britney was telling Harper that she was crazy to dance with me, and I was pretty sure there would be some price to pay. Harper just laughed and kept tugging me out to the dance floor.

"See, you're not the only brave one," she said, and she had to move in close to me so that I would hear her. I'm pretty sure her lips touched my ear.

Not quite in the kiss category, but it had to count for something.

"No, you're definitely brave to dance with someone who moves like this!" I said, and we both laughed and took our place with the rest of Hickory Hills.

THE END

ABOUT THE AUTHOR

After 20 years as a middle school English teacher, Re Marzullo has seen it all and lived to tell (and write) about it. She enjoys reading on her back porch and eating peanut butter out of the jar. After a childhood spent as an Army brat and moving every two years, she now lives in suburban Atlanta with her family.

Connect with Re Marzullo at:

twitter.com/remarz
facebook.com/spedrules
remarzullo.wordpress.com

SPED2
CHAPTER ONE

When I was little I heard the saying that the "grass wasn't always greener on the other side" and thought it meant something about fertilizer or maybe mowing the lawn so your neighbors wouldn't get mad.

Now I knew better.

What the saying really meant was that maybe you should appreciate your own grass and not always be wishing for your neighbor's. It also meant that when you wished for something *really* badly for a *really* long time and then FINALLY got it, it may not be so great after all.

In fact, it (whatever it is you had wanted for such a long time) may be a lot harder than you thought it would be, and you may wish (with all your heart) that you had stayed on your own grass!

Unfortunately, I found out a little too late that my grass was (maybe) greener and now I'm (definitely) stuck without a mower or even a weed whacker and the lawn is getting pretty high.

Here's the deal...I, Jack Parker, cruised through sixth and seventh grade in the Special Education or SPED slow lane. SPED was for kids like me with learning problems. My problem happened to be dyslexia – when I read, the letters got flipped and flopped and it took me some time to figure the words out – and so I got put in SPED back in elementary school.

Since my writing wasn't affected, it took my old teachers a minute to realize that I was totally faking my way through story time, but once they gave me tests and junk it was pretty obvious that I had a learning disability.

Elementary school SPED was no big deal since a teacher would just come into the class and give me extra help in reading. No muss, no fuss, and I was able to keep up pretty well.

That changed once I got to Hickory Hills Middle School, HHMS, where they put *all* the SPED kids in a class called Small Group Superstars (don't laugh) or SGS. It was for sure a Small Group, and we had just a few of us in a room with our teacher Ms. McFee.

Same room, same kids, same teacher all day long.

That was my old grass.

When it came out that the principal Mr. Feathers was just keeping all of us SPED kids in small group so that his state test scores would be higher (not cool, Feathers), the board of education freaked out, forced

Feathers to retire, and a decision was made to move us all into "regular" classes for the rest of eighth grade.

That's my new grass.

A part of me was excited to be getting out of SGS and taking "regular" classes. I knew that being in regular classes in middle school led to regular classes in high school. That was important because some day I wanted to go college (I want to be a forensic scientist when I grow up), but I had to admit that I was kind of scared.

Of many things.

First, I was scared of being the "new kid" in all of my classes. After two years of SGS, I was only "new" on the first day of sixth grade and after that it was the same kids every day.

Since there were only seven of us in SGS, calling roll took about a half a second on a slow day.

Here's the former SGS roster (not in alphabetical order, sorry McFee):

Xinho Park, an Asian kid who unfortunately for him was not your typical Asian brainiac and one of my best friends. Leo Delaney, a little dude who used to be an easy target for all the HHMS bullies, but was enjoying a little peace now that he had Bernie Massey in his corner.

Bernie's a tough girl who was put into SPED and SGS after she moved in with a foster family in our school district. Luckily, though, Bernie now lives with Ms. McFee, our old SPED teacher. Way cool how that worked out.

There's also Bryce Williams, the Incredible Bulk, who became a hero a couple of months ago when he beat our school's resident bully Colin Markus in the FunRun, and Skeever Rowlings who was a typical ADD kid and couldn't sit still for 30 seconds. Skeevs had a joke for every occasion and made everyone laugh.

Lastly was Harper Noble.

Ahhhh, Harper.

She was a new girl (rare in these parts) at the beginning of the school year who had the misfortune of being exiled to SPED-ville with all of us. I had a massive crush on Harper the Beautiful for the first half of the year, though now we were friends.

"Just friends" as she told anyone who asked.

Oh well.

When I started eighth grade this year, I didn't have any friends or people that I hung out with outside of school (my parents didn't count) but now I do, so I think that I'm making progress.

Who cared if I all of my friends were SPED-heads like me from SGS? We were buds, and now I was worried that we wouldn't have any classes together.

So that's another thing I'm scared of.

To recap...

Scary Thing One: being a new kid in all my classes.

Scary Thing Two: not having any SPED friends in my classes.

Biggest Scary Thing of All: keeping up with the workload in my new classes.

I'm terrified that the work will be too hard, and I'll get bad grades and never get into college, which was the reason I wanted out of SGS in the first place!

Anyway, after fighting with the principal and the school board about getting into regular classes, I was wondering if I should have just stayed in my safe SPED class.

Long story not very short, that's what I meant about the grass.

All of this junk had been hanging over my head during the entire Christmas break. Two weeks of no school was great, but two weeks of dreading school was terrible.

So now Christmas break was over, school started tomorrow, and I was wide awake at two in the morning worrying about my lawn.

CPSIA information can be obtained
at www.ICGtesting.com
Printed in the USA
FFOW04n1521250414
5054FF

9 780988 961807